Taming the Divine Heron

Taming the Divine Heron

SERGIO PITOL

Translated from the Spanish by G. B. Henson

DEEP VELLUM PUBLISHING

DALLAS, TEXAS

Deep Vellum Publishing
3000 Commerce St., Dallas, Texas 75226
deepvellum.org · @deepvellum

Deep Vellum is a 501c3 nonprofit literary arts organization
founded in 2013 with the mission to bring
the world into conversation through literature.

Support for this publication has been provided in part by the National Endowment for the
Arts, the Texas Commission on the Arts, the City of Dallas Office of Arts and Culture, and
the George and Fay Young Foundation.

ISBNs: 978-1-64605-276-9 (paperback) | 978-1-64605-297-4 (ebook)

LIBRARY OF CONGRESS CATALOGING-IN-PUBLICATION DATA
Names: Pitol, Sergio, 1933-2018, author. | Henson, George, translator.
Title: Taming the divine heron / Sergio Pitol ; translated from the Spanish
by George Henson.
Other titles: Domar a la divina garza. English
Description: First US edition. | Dallas, Texas : Deep Vellum Publishing,
2023. | Sequel to: The love parade.
Identifiers: LCCN 2023023618 (print) | LCCN 2023023619 (ebook) | ISBN
9781646052769 (trade paperback) | ISBN 9781646052974 (epub)
Subjects: LCGFT: Novels.
Classification: LCC PQ7298.26.I8 D6613 2023 (print) | LCC PQ7298.26.I8
(ebook) | DDC 863/.64--dc23/eng/20230524
LC record available at https://lccn.loc.gov/2023023618
LC ebook record available at https://lccn.loc.gov/2023023619

Front Cover Design by Kit Schluter
Interior Layout and Typesetting by KGT

Printed in Canada

For Juan García Ponce

Taming the ~~Queen Bee~~ Divine Heron

Translation is a funny thing. Like a puzzle or riddle, sometimes the solution is obvious. More often than not, however, it's seldom clear cut. We translators work in a liminal space rife with ambiguity and polysemy, where metaphors and idioms in the source language regularly have scant or no equivalence in the target language. The best we can do, well, is do our best.

Titles are one of the translator's many bugaboos. Curiously, while the title may be the last thing the writer writes, it is the first thing the reader reads. A title is never incidental. Never trivial. It is suggestive. It insinuates. It creates anticipation. It piques the reader's interest. It sets a mood.

Which brings me to the title of the novel in your hand—*Domar a la divina garza*—which I've translated literally as *Taming the Divine Heron*. A Spanish reader—especially one from Mexico—would connect with it immediately. The idiom gained particular currency when, in a not-so-friendly spar with María Félix, the queen bee of Mexico's Golden Age of Cinema, famous for her witty and often catty one-liners, television host Paco Malgesto asked the diva if she thought herself the divine heron, to which Félix, without batting a false eyelash, responded: *Yo no me creo la divina garza. ¡Yo soy la divina garza!* (I don't think I'm the divine heron. I am the divine heron!).

The English reader, on the other hand, is left to divine (excuse the pun) its meaning, hoping to make a connection as they read. By translating the title literally, in addition to losing something in translation, the idiom also runs the risk of being lost on readers. Hence this note.

As is often the case, the difficulty in translating *Domar a la divina garza* lies in maintaining the allusion to a popular idiom: *creerse la divina garza* (to believe oneself the divine heron). Of uncertain origin, it's roughly equivalent to "believing oneself the queen bee" or, more crudely, "hot shit," which might have been appropriate considering the scatological thread that runs through the novel.

So why, you may be wondering, did I not choose one of the aforementioned English equivalents? Thankfully, my always generous and ever-astute publisher, Will Evans, who has always allowed me free rein in almost every regard, put the kibosh on *Taming the Queen Bee*. Or why did I not, like the French translator, who titled the novel *Mater la divine garce* (taming the divine bitch), choose a title that approximates the idiom's meaning, even at the expense of a cultural loss? I did consider, briefly, *Taming the Divine Shrew*, but the allusion to Shakespeare, I concluded, would impose gratuitous (distracting?) intertextuality on the text (although something tells me that Pitol, who borrowed from Shakespeare freely, might have liked it). Always irreverent, I even suspect he would chuckle at a title as playful as *Taming the Divine Beetch*.

As you read, it will become clear that the novel's protagonist, Dante de la Estrella, like Paco Malgesto, is truly on a mission to tame his divine heron. And I hope that, perhaps, after you've finished, you'll make the idiom your own. English will only be richer for it. After all, isn't that the aim of translation?

G.B. Henson

Tulsa, OK

I

Wherein an aging novelist, haunted by the approach of old age, reveals his craft and reflects on the materials with which he intends to construct a new novel.

AN AGING WRITER IS PREPARING to begin a new novel. He reads, with scant enthusiasm at first, then with frank indifference, bits and pieces of two or three paragraphs from a chapter, beset by a feeling very close to anguish; he closes the volume wishing to never open it again during the remaining days of his life. He recalls a comment made by Carlos Montiel, the literary critic, a friend of his since their college days, who, after reading his first stories, told him that some of the characters too closely resembled certain decidedly ordinary classmates from university: young men capable of everything except living a tragedy, disqualified from embodying the subtleties and a Jamesian sort of chiaroscuro, to whom, however, he strove to provide a byzantine emotional complexity, a realm nourished by intense aesthetic messianisms, behavior that was alien to such a degree that rather than giving them life it deprived them of it. The rarefied atmosphere that enveloped them became their prison; having succumbed, they became incapable of freeing themselves from engaging in conversation and behaving like ventriloquists' dummies.

If he believed Montiel, and the recent unpleasant reading confirmed his words, everything he'd written until then was intimately and irredeemably condemned. His literature had no future; it had been anachronistic already at the moment of its birth. He was about to turn sixty-five. A cruel age! At times he thinks that what he truly longed for was to rest on the withered laurels he'd earned, to repeat the limited range of already proven techniques until they became completely expended, to keep a more or less plausible language alive until the urge was extinguished by natural causes. His is an age, this he knows, in which one might also run the risk of being trampled by an intricate network of inner movements, projection, a scope and development so vast, so densely obscure, that they exceed the possibilities of creation; to feel shaken by a fury, a violence that exceeds everything; to fall in love with long-awaited emotions and, one day, suddenly, abandon forever that project suddenly revealed to be an immense folly. To finally begin the ambitious work about which one has dreamt all one's life, for which one has collected over the years an enormous amount of information and details, a book teeming with sound and fury that would redeem one's own existence and justify it to the world? At his age, such a feat takes on the glint of an immense blunder. Failing to achieve the long-dreamt glory sought in another time doesn't necessarily have to be a tragedy. The end isn't far off, and the book in question would require years of research and sustained work. To bring upon oneself such mistreatment when one already has so little energy, looming old age, and its attendant infirmities, and then leave a novel half finished? No, really, thank you very much!

His heroes know only two paths, both mechanical, incidentally, to access fiction, that is to say, their novelistic reality. They've returned from a rich life experience, inexplicably fractured, which forces them to hide away either in some town in Morelos, or they're in a small city in Veracruz, where, dejected, withered, overcome with resentment, they gradually bleed themselves dry: the heroines shed their petals against a sepia background, fondling old letters, yellowed photographs, newspaper clippings from years ago, and remember, remember and remember, those feverish beings they once were, and still others, those who clutched them in their arms, intoxicated them with fiery words, and then, for a reason always unknown, expelled them from their lives. During their boyhood all his male characters longed to be Lord Jim, Alyosha Karamazov, Fabrizio del Dongo. They had all lived through a period of ephemeral brilliance, interrupted by tragedy. If by chance they survived the fall, these protagonists would return, driven by an apparent thirst for identity, to their places of origin, to enjoy, if that could be the verb, a little house in the sun, next to a small garden with a smattering of flowers. Córdoba, Cuernavaca, San Andrés Tuxtla, Huatusco, Tepoztlán, and Cuautla are a few of the places chosen by this human waste as a refuge to end their days. Shortly after returning to the coveted Eden, they will discover they've fallen into a pit from which escape is impossible, that they've allowed themselves to become trapped, that those who wished them ill have ultimately triumphed by ridding themselves of them, that they're surrounded by traitors, by disloyal and envious people. And there they'll grow old, burdened with all matter of ills, debts, and manias, intoxicated with rancor toward a world incapable of appreciating them, bewildered by the nothings they've ultimately become. Old, neurotic creatures, at times droll but mostly bitter, resentful, with no way out, no future, no recourse.

But these protagonists could be considered successful compared to those in the latter category, those who weren't able to return to those sunlit houses and to their tiny orchards, those whom life ensnared in much less generous latitudes. They wander around the world, having been forgotten by everyone and forgetting everything. Did they even try to return? Were they not able? They didn't quite know. Behold them: night watchmen in a damp cellar, in some wooden storehouse, in a parking lot, doormen in cheap hotels, beneficiaries of some philanthropic institution that finds these fates for them to make them feel useful and to help them recover a modicum of their lost dignity. Forgotten by everyone in their own country, absolute strangers where they live. It's possible that their circumstances haven't always been this way. They too must have known a summer or two of initial happiness. With whom had they danced? What step could have been fatal for them? Dirty and toothless, they scarcely notice how quickly their memory is fading. Their revenge consists precisely in that, in shutting down all the channels that connect them with the past. If someone tried to remind them of the shock they lived through thirty years ago, the inner turmoil they experienced when they stood before Giorgione's *The Tempest* or the *Sleeping Venus*, the consecutive visits over four days to the pavilion that housed the Matisse exhibition at the Venice Biennale, where each time they left inebriated with joy and wonder, or the somber days spent in a boarding house while they pieced together the dreadful fate of Adrian Leverkühn and shuddered at the blot that stained the soul of the faithful Serenus as he revealed it, they would sketch an obscene sign, hurl a gob of spit at the feet of the interlocutor, that stranger who feigned familiarity, who approached them suddenly with open arms and that inexplicable language, and they'd immediately run away, slipping through a labyrinth of putrid alleyways until reaching the hovel where they spend the night; they'd lie down on a dirty mattress, covered from head to toe with an equally dirty blanket, trembling, their bodies bathed in thick sweat, longing only for the arrival of sleep that would restore their peace. In reality, the only thing that interests them is to not be expelled from the hole where they spend their days and to remember the time and place where they must stand, bowl in hand, at the hot soup window. The trenchant Montiel, he recalls, was absolutely right. If he wanted to continue, he had to start by getting rid of some bad habits and toss all that useless junk into the fire. But would there still be time to frequent new spaces?

How could he forget that he was on the eve of his sixty-fifth birthday?

Perhaps the most important thing was to decide where to start. He had a series of references, still very confusing, so vague that they seemed to vanish the minute they were born, or transform into something else. It became essential to begin to pinpoint some of those images: an encounter in Istanbul, a learned woman with rather unconventional manners and language, the sordidness of a cheapskate, an indisputably barbaric celebration in a clearing in the jungle of Tabasco.

He finally decided to sketch some notes. Three subjects, for different reasons, had interested him recently, which, in some vague way, connected the encounter in Istanbul with the outrages committed by the cheapskate and the feast in the tropics.

He wrote the following on large notecards:

A) Bakhtin's book on popular culture in the Middle Ages and early Renaissance! Focus on certain elements: the Feast, for example, as a primary and indestructible category of human civilization. The notion of the feast can become impoverished, even degenerate, but not completely eclipsed. Without the feast, which liberates and redeems, man gestures in a mere simulacrum of life. To study the relationship between the ceremonial, the mystic, and the feast in primitive as well as contemporary industrial societies. Catholicism and, perhaps more still, the Byzantine church, as communicating bridges between us and the pagan roots of the ancient feast, incorporating certain characteristics of popular revelry into ritual forms while allowing others to develop with absolute freedom, outside the cult, etc., etc., etc.

B) Gogol! Bakhtin perceives the carnivalesque breath as a fundamental support of the complex Gogolian verbal organism. An almost exacerbated, one might say, reading of this Russian's work and that of his exegetes. Few writers in our century have relied on commentators of such exceptional quality: Boris Eikhenbaum, V. V. Gippius, Andrei Bely, Vladimir Nabokov, Andrei Sinyavsky, etc. Symbolists, formalists, dissidents of all orthodoxies converge in him. A temptation to attempt a short text on a theme from *Dead Souls*. To piece together why Chichikov, the protagonist, whom the author presents from the opening paragraph as an absolute nonentity ("he was not handsome, but neither was he particularly bad-looking; he was neither too fat, nor too thin; he could not be said to be too old, but he was not too young either"), as a character with no personal characteristics of any kind, who manages to make all those he encounters become full, at his sole contact, of life. His existence illuminates that of others and, at the same time, is nourished by the very life that his presence fosters. Even in the second part of *Dead Souls*, in the tedious fragments that survive, the mere appearance of Chichikov manages to overcome the moralizing tenor that paralyzes many of its pages and returns to them something of the air that every work of fiction needs to breathe. Wherever the scoundrel puts his hand, an illumination is suddenly produced, not light from the sun but the sort that comes from a footlight, stage light that bathes a character and makes him lose his earthliness, deforms him, reduces him, and manages to extract from him his true physiognomy. More than an essay, this could be used in the novel. My protagonist's rapaciousness provides little, but his sordidness could be useful, like Chichikov's nonexistent virtues, in illuminating the behavior of other characters and, at the same time, could be enriched in return.

C) Pepe Brozas or the almost religious unction that a certain author can arouse in people lacking the slightest affinity for the arts! Remembering the case of José Rosas, a classmate from law school, whom, shortly after his admission, all the students came to know by the nickname "Pepe Brozas," a not-so-subtle reference to his humble origins. Originally from Piedras Negras, he attended preparatory school in Mexico City then went on to study law. He spent two years in Rome, if I remember correctly, on scholarship, trying in vain to obtain a doctorate. He held a position in the International Affairs Directorate of some State Secretariat, which allowed him to take trips abroad. He adopted airs that feigned cosmopolitanism, with which he failed to hide the idiotic way in which he radically and exuberantly invented nuances. It's impossible to imbue him with subtleties or refined concerns! An unadulterated rube! He never ceased to be the same lout, but he became solemn and pompous and, thus, even more intolerable. In the end he got rich managing his wife's properties in Cuernavaca. The money, his need to flaunt it, and his passion for keeping it heightened his vulgarity. A single feature set him apart. His passion for Dante. Yes, Dante Alighieri, the Florentine. Yes, yes, the author of *The Divine Comedy*. He'd studied Italian in preparatory school, which was the origin of this peculiarity.

He would read it, reread it, expound on it, although, of course, in a grotesque fashion; in a way, he considered it his own property. Yet he remained the most reluctant sort for any kind of literary excitement. By the way, go through old notes from Berlin. Perhaps I'll manage to find some notes on that German who resembled Rosas . . . Matthias . . . Glaubner? Matthias Glaubner or Glaubener. A young economics graduate from the School of Foreign Trade, where he'd specialized in trade relations with Latin America. He spoke impeccable Spanish. In his spare time he accepted jobs from a number of university institutions as a translator and interpreter. It's hard to think of anyone more tedious than that German boy. Petty interests, obtuse nationalism! What a pain to be roped into going to exhibitions, concerts, or theatrical performances with him! The inanity of his comments made one lose all interest in conversing with him. Making money, buying on the cheap, saving money were the only visible concerns in his life. One day, in the midst of the usual stream of platitudes, he repeated a quotation from Calvino's *Invisible Cities,* which led to an almost inconceivable story. Glaubner had learned Italian, which wasn't a required language in his studies, just to be able to read Italo Calvino in his own language. As unusual as it may seem, he knew his entire oeuvre to perfection. A Spanish teacher had lent him, years ago, an Argentine edition of *The Path to the Nest of Spiders.* He began to read it with ennui, merely to enrich his vocabulary. Suddenly, something in the reading touched an unexpected place in his being and lit a fire. He discovered that a novel could be something other than a tedious enumeration of social or psychologizing fripperies, capable of transmitting to him something that had nothing to do with what he conceptualized as literature, producing emotions known only in his treaties on foreign trade and statistics, and perhaps even more intense. That day a kind of mystical union took place between the student from Berlin and the Italian author. He continued to read Calvino, no longer in Spanish but in German, while learning Italian. He read the critical notes that accompanied the appearance of "his" author in Germany. In the letters to the editor section of some newspapers of no importance he refuted, with the most abstruse arguments, several of those reviews. This passion for Calvino did not, however, open the doors to other fields, nor did it enrich his curiosity or broaden the radius of his thinking, nor did it pique his interest in any other author. Those readings didn't connect him to anything; they didn't expand or reduce any concept— they exhausted themselves. But they did fulfill a need that was real, that one might consider spiritual for lack of a more appropriate adjective. The same thing happened to Rosas with Dante. He knew everything about him yet understood nothing.

What a treasure, a character like Pepe Brozas! Alongside his vulgarity, coarseness, selfishness, greed, and rapaciousness stood a heroic, disinterested passion for the work of a distant writer. In the novel, he'd cease to be Dante and become Gogol. To contaminate, if possible, the language with some of the Russian's verbal eccentricity. The passion for Gogol could have been introduced by someone with a certain resemblance to that rather queer Greek ethnologist who recently gave a pair of lectures at the University on the Mesoamerican works of her late husband. Find an exotic name for her in order to lend a certain comicalness. An intensely individual character who embodies the feast and before whom Brozas's sad rapaciousness is always defeated.

●

The aging novelist who engages our attention, fatigued and insecure, began the second half of the sixth decade of his life writing
a new novel: *Taming the Divine Heron.* In it he would intertwine
his three fundamental themes: the feast, that "primary and indestructible category of civilization," that magical space where the
differences between men become blurred and disappear; he would
exorcise the old ghost of his youth, the loathsome Brozas from his
school days, and he would renew his passion for Gogol. Led by a
foreigner of uncertain nationality, Professor Marietta Karapetiz,
the protagonist will penetrate with absolute confidence, without
losing his air of perpetual hallucination, the Gogolian labyrinth,
from which he will escape only when he learns years later of his
mentor's death. Meeting Marietta Karapetiz, talking to her and her
brother Alexander—Sacha to his closest friends—was, although
he may not have known it, although he may refuse to believe it,
the most important event of his life. Guided by Marietta's hand,
like Alighieri by Virgil, José Rosas, who in the novel will be called
Dante de la Estrella, in homage, one could say, to his enthusiasm
for the Florentine bard, will sense the fragrance of a tropical feast
held at the beginning of our century. The experience will be so
intense that even in his old age the main character will strain his
memory to explain it. Describing that struggle and some of its circumstances is the mission the aging writer intends to accomplish
in this hypothetical next novel.

II

Wherein the author narrates the sundry adventures of Dante C. de la Estrella, Esq., bordering, in the author's judgment, on the picaresque, which culminated in a trip to Istanbul.

AND SO, BY THE WILL and grace of a novelist, Dante C. de la Estrella, Esq., found himself one rainy afternoon in Tepoztlán, sitting in the middle of a comfortable black leather sofa in Salvador Millares's den. He leafs through some newspapers, not so much without conviction as with indifference; uncomfortable, it seems, since no one in the house pays him the attention of which he considers himself deserving. The architect is engrossed in reading a novel, by Simenon, to be precise. His father, Don Antonio Millares, is playing an exceedingly complicated game of solitaire with four decks of cards that prevents him from paying attention to anything other than the game table. His sister Amelia is crocheting a tablecloth of very fine pearl-colored yarn. Millares's children, Juan Ramón and Elena, are each working diligently at the big table, assembling jigsaw puzzles.

A storm had been threatening since noon. The large picture window that looks out onto the mountain suddenly lit up. A roar, a thundering explosion of light. A tree of sparks fell on Tepozteco, extending its phosphorescence, with each passing instant, to renewed, trembling branches, until covering in an otherworldly way the entire window. One discharge, another, then others, one after another, as if in a chain reaction.

"The fainthearted are more often affected by thunder than by lightning. Isn't that strange?" De la Estrella exclaimed, his voice on edge. "There are those who begin to howl when they hear it. I've witnessed it. They howl and howl and don't stop; they howl until they lose their mind. Thank you, God, for the extraordinary strength you've given me! With me by your side, you can rest at ease."

For a good while everyone had been silent. The voice that uttered these words seemed to make a greater impression on those present than any manifestation of the storm. Amelia Millares left the crochet basket in her bergère and walked out of the room, only to return a short time later, accompanied by a servant, with two oil lamps that they placed on a desk, just in case. One never knew what could happen during a thunderstorm, even less so when, as on that day, it was unleashed with such violence. As she placed the lamps strategically, she commented that she hoped it wouldn't occur to Julia to leave Mexico City in such weather.

"I hate to think of her at this hour in the car, unable to see the road."

The architect Salvador Millares walked to the telephone and dialed a number. He waited a few moments with the receiver at his ear. No one answered. It was strange, as there was always someone at his mother-in-law's house at that hour. He returned to his chair and, before resuming his novel, he thought for a moment about his wife's most recent inexplicable whims. Leaving the house at all hours. For years, she'd insisted on leaving the capital to live in the country. But from the moment they settled permanently in Tepoztlán she'd spent most of her time in the city. She'd accepted a series of absurd jobs. Whatever they offered her, indiscriminately, as if a newly discovered greed had overcome her. She'd been behaving this way for almost half a year. Julia's sudden decision to work, to abandon her former idle habits, continued to amaze him. Interior architecture, remodeling, decorating, that sort of thing, together with her mother. 'Very well!' he said to himself, rankled, and, as he looked at his guest, the rancor became more pronounced. He could understand everything, except that she would accept a job he'd refused, and that she'd do it for De la Estrella, whom they both knew very well, an unscrupulous huckster, a complete shyster, with whom she'd certainly clash a few days after starting the work. She'd spend more time collecting her fees than redoing his house. Salvador Millares had worked with him fourteen or fifteen years before, on a real estate development on the outskirts of Cuernavaca. From that time he remembers only petty attitudes, spiritual miserliness, braggadocio, threats. An absolutely immature, resentful and, therefore, dangerous sort. He wasn't yet living in Tepoztlán. The house was but a small cabin, suitable only for weekends. The Licenciado would show up every Saturday morning so they could go together to the development to check on the construction. Millares found him unlikable from the first day, but he never imagined that things would end so badly. He didn't even remember how the partnership began, who introduced them, only that De la Estrella had just started in the construction business. And it was the first major contract he'd received as an architect. He was surprised when De la Estrella had suggested recently, first by phone, then during a personal visit, that he undertake some renovations to his house in Cuernavaca. He wanted to take advantage of the time his wife was going to spend with their daughter and son-in-law somewhere near the border. He found his obstinacy off-putting. Millares of course refused, so De la Estrella approached his mother-in-law, who passed the project on to Julia. Of course she also refused the request. What unnecessary nonsense the whole affair! What an outrageous lack of tact to show up at his house and insist that his wife take over the work, to demand to talk to her in person, to sit in his living room, to impose his presence for so long! He'd greeted him coldly, pointed to a seat, and gestured to a basket that held the latest newspapers and magazines.Had he not been taken by surprise, he wouldn't have even allowed him to come in. He hadn't the slightest desire to converse with him and pretend that nothing serious had happened between them. What had happened indeed! First a series of insinuations questioning his honesty regarding the budget; then, half in earnest, half in jest, he'd begun to threaten a lawsuit, to take him to court if he didn't reduce the agreed-upon fees. He had to accept. The twins had already been born, and he had few offers of employment. He became furious again. He approached him after hanging up the phone and rather dryly said:

"Look, Licenciado, I'm afraid my wife will be in Mexico City until tomorrow. I don't want to waste your time. If you're going to return to Cuernavaca, I'd suggest you do so before it getsdark. Before long the road will be impassable."

After saying those words, andwithout waitingfor a response, he returned to his armchair,picked up the detective novel, and tried, with considerable effort, to concentrate on it.

"I understand your concern for my welfare, Millares," De la Estrella replied pettishly. "I understand and appreciate it for what it's worth. Rest assured that as soon as this storm subsides I'll leave. Perhaps sooner. My driver has gone to Santiago Tepetlapa; I expect him back to pick me up in about half an hour. Don't worry about

me. Continue to cultivate yourself; reading's never harmed anyone, unless one spends one's time on minor genres. I know some
who've never been able to overcome their addiction to them." And
he stared at the architect with a peevish frown curdled on his lips.

As soon as De la Estrella entered the house, Millares had
noticed a certain frenzied look on his face. An extreme facial tension, as if he were about to suffer some kind of crisis, strange gestures, a nervous tic of the neck; he tilted his head to one side, like
some frantic animals in the moment just before they pounce. The
gaze had an abnormal fixedness. The brown of his eyes seemed to
break into tiny yellow and reddish striations. De la Estrella fixed his
stare into a corner for a few minutes. Then he took his hands to the
collar of his shirt, grabbed the knot of his tie, attempted to loosen
it, but didn't succeed, or perhaps he changed his mind. With a sib-
ylline voice he said again, in a mocking singsong:

"You've been kind enough, Millares, to state a truth the size of
a cathedral. One must always remember that time is the greatest
treasure we possess and cannot be foolishly wasted. Time, to whoever possesses, is like pearls that must be kept far from the voracious snout of swine . . ." He rose with visible effort, took a few
steps, and added: "Before I close any deal with your wife, we must
agree on a series of factors; the type of materials to be used, the
costs, the timeline to complete the work, and not only on the decorative aspects, which are of the least interest to me. I know women; I
know how given they are to extravagance, waste, and squandering.
I don't want any surprises."

He approached the table where Juan Ramón and Elena,
Millares's twin children, had been working on their puzzles since
the beginning of the afternoon. Elena was about to finish the
Taj Mahal, while Juan Ramón was struggling to give shape to a

minaret. There were several blank spaces on the board, but it was already possible to recognize the outlines of the Blue Mosque. The Licenciado De la Estrella became paralyzed as he contemplated the work in progress, his head tilted even more to the right, his stare more glazed, his neck more tense. One would have thought that at any moment he might begin to foam at the mouth.

"There are ten famous artistic monuments," explained Juan Ramón, who was unaware of the change suffered by the strange visitor. "The Taj Mahal, Notre Dame, the Church of Saint Basil in Moscow, the Duomo of Milan, the Cathedral of Cologne, the Palace of Versailles, the Castle of Chapultepec, the Alhambra in Granada. This is the Blue Mosque in Istanbul, one of the most difficult."

"We've finished more than half of it. At the beginning it took a lot of effort. You don't know . . . ," Elena started to say, but the Licenciado didn't allow her to finish.

"I've seen many of these monuments," he said in a shrill voice. "Sometimes it's necessary for me to say this, to remind the world, so that it knows, if it hasn't already realized, withwhom it's speaking."

"Juan Ramón's is the hardest," Elena insisted again. "That and the Alhambra, which is awfully hard. It's called the Blue Mosque. Constantinople is now called Istanbul."

"I stood in front of the Blue Mosque for a moment. I've stood before several things; today I don't know whether I saw them or not. I, the man with the sharpest memory in the world, do not remember if I stopped to contemplate this or that monument or if I walked past them." And with a voice whose sound resembled glass scraping glass, he continued: "It was in Istanbul, the ancient Constantinople, as you say, that I met one of the greatest impostors in history. A living fraud who called herself Marietta Karapetiz, to whom I, if I were to refer solely to her manners, would give the name, if you will excuse me, Pellagra Slutanova. In places of less than dubious morals, she was known by the nom de guerre of Little Hands of Satin. I don't know if you've heard of her, or if you've read the series of articles in which I took it upon myself to put her in her rightful place."

"Whom did you meet?" asked Salvador Millares's father, just to say something.

"Marietta Karapetiz, if that was her real name, which I believe unlikely, whom in my dreams and reveries I'm accustomed to calling Pellagra Slutanova. Her brother, and other gentlemen of great families, but only God knows of what customs, used to call her Little Hands of Satin," said the Licenciado in a single breath, wiping his enormous, sweat-drenched forehead with a dirty handkerchief, apparently forgetting his immediate offenses. He spoke as if he were playing a part he'd learned to perfection but performed with notorious clumsiness. He'd stand up only to immediately sit down again, move his arms and hands wildly, gesticulate. The only thing immobile was his fixed gaze and the tilting of his face to his right side. "Yes, my friends, I am referring to that celebrated and hardened *habituée* of the seediest of banquets, the most repulsive of feasts, and the most unbridled of orgies, and who, nevertheless, went about the world vaunting the strictest of academic pedigrees. Rigor in the flesh! What a laughingstock! Everything about her was a farce. Both brother and sister had frequented since their youth circles that reached a degree of licentiousness that not even Nero could have imagined. Hands of Satin! Steel Grip! I must admit that I never knew Sacha's ultimate fate. I've neglected that detail. I don't know if he followed his sister on her journey to Avernus, or if in some hospice for the elderly in some remote place in this world, orphaned by his sister, he's trying by means of the Ouija board to make contact with the blackness of her soul. The farther one stays away from those people, the better! To hell with them!" He snorted loudly. He knows he's triumphed once again, that he's succeeded in surprising the enemy. He's forced them all, young and old alike, to look up from their contemptible diversions; he's forced them to recognize that he exists. That he is who he is! Dante C. de la Estrella, Esq.! And this misstep, this curiosity, will end up losing the Millareses. Like it or not, the unwelcome guest won't leave the house until he's finished his story. If he were so inclined, he could force them to listen to the wonders of the remarkable Gogol, deliver a short lecture, dumbfound them, enlighten them a bit, force them to recognize his intellectual superiority. Everything would come in due time! With the exaltation of a madman, he continued: "It was mid-1961 when I traveled to Istanbul. It was August, and Europe was experiencing one of the worst heat waves in recorded history. That August in Rome, feet were sinking into the pavement. Walking had become more than exhausting: to unstick a shoe, only to sink it back into the soft, thin asphalt layer that covered the Roman streets, then start over again, and so on ad infinitum. Never mind Istanbul! I was finishing a doctorate in constitutional law in Rome. The story isn't to be believed: my presence in the eternal city, as much the result of chance as if I'd participated in a lottery whose jackpot was a trip to Italy! My brother-in-law Antonio had found out by chance about the existence of a scholarship to study at the University of Rome, and at the appropriate moment arranged to have it awarded to me. One of the greatest talents of world literature, a Russian incidentally, the immortal Nikolai Vasilyevich Gogol, once wrote that by a strange order of things, alien to man's comprehension, trivial causes often result in great events, just as, to the contrary, sometimes the greatest undertakings end in less than trivial results. My worldly experience has taught me to acknowledge that no greater truth than this has ever been spoken. My brother-in-law, I must admit, why shouldn't I, was a real piece of work, a profligate ne'er-do-well, of whom I had the worst impression since exchanging my first words with him. My sister Blanca—a name that has nothing, I wish to clarify from the start, to do with the color of her soul, thanks to a clumsiness since childhood that characterized her in everything, and to say "everything" is the same as saying everything that is insignificant, because she never experienced a single major event in her life—discovered some years after the marriage the kind of a scoundrel her husband was and immediately proceeded to file for divorce. There were money matters pending between them. He'd sold, for example, an apartment they owned together and hadn't given Blanca the half that was owed to her. After the separation, Blanca went to live in Guadalajara. She refused to stay in the capital because she detested it; she hated it from the moment she set foot there, but nor did she want to return to Piedras Negras either, because, according to her, it made her nervous to arrive alone and announce to the city that her marriage had been a disaster, as if anyone would be interested there or anywhere else in Blanca's successes or failures. She went so far as to tell me, and this truly was laughable, that she wouldn't return because her friends didn't have the same intellect as she did and that it would be difficult for her to talk about the subjects that interested her. As if she'd ever talked about anything other than rumors and gossip! Now, why she chose Guadalajara as her destination remains a real mystery to me. The only thing she was interested in at the time was finalizing the divorce and recovering the money from the apartment that was sold. One of my sister's peculiarities has always been her inability to keep her affairs in order. They weren't married under the community property regime, and she'd lost I don't know what documents without which she couldn't prove that she'd paid for half of the apartment; without them it would be difficult to recover the disputed funds. She phoned me and delegated me to take care of the matter. In order to recover the documents, very likely purloined by the former man in her life before the separation occurred, we could raise one hell of a scandal that would make the former husband believe that the position he'd recently secured in the government office of the Federal District, about which he was very smug, was in danger of going down the drain. It would be a serious miscalculation on his part, said Blanca, not to live up to his commitments, as she believed he'd get much more—much, much more!—from that position than he'd received from the sale of their joint property. We had to threaten him with revealing to the press certain details about his life that she knew to a T. This was the only way we'd be able to force him to consider the matter. Antonio was stubborn and a hard nut to crack; we knew that, but there was nothing to lose by trying. My sister offered me ten percent of whatever I managed to recover. I didn't accept; she raised it to fifteen, and I replied, to get her off my back, without committing myself to anything, that I'd feel my brother-in-law out. I called him. He made an appointment with me at the Rendezvous, a rather pleasant café on the Paseo de la Reforma, I don't know if you remember it. It occupied the first floor of a dark glass building, one of the first skyscrapers, you might say, on the Reforma. To my surprise, Antonio greeted me with smiles and pats on the back. Antonio Pérez was his full name; not at all bright, if you will allow me to digress. And if you forced me, I'd tell you that his second surname was García." He let out a dry, caw-like laugh, without the slightest joy. "As I said, as soon as he saw me, he stood up with a smile from ear to ear. 'I'm screwed now,' I said to myself, 'if he's brought witnesses, he feels very confident,' but on second thought, 'or maybe it's the other way around. If he's brought witnesses, it means he doesn't feel confident at all and is trying to fool me, perhaps intimidate me.' He got up when he saw me approach his table; he gave me a hug as if we were on the best of terms, introduced me to his friends; he told them plainly, and I had the impression that on that occasion he was sincere: 'This fellow, my brother-in-law, has just finished his law degree in the most brilliant way. He devoted himself to his studies, and I predict a brilliant future for him. As he faces the beginning of his career, that crucial moment in all our lives, where, as the great Hobbes said, every man becomes a wolf to man, Dante deserves all the attention and help that can be afforded him.' He began almost immediately to talk about a scholarship that someone in his office had mentioned to do graduate studies in Rome; the circumstances were perfect, the only thing that was needed was the approval of the Secretary of Education. 'I'd appreciate it, Iglesias,' he said to one of his companions, 'since you work there, if you'd give him a hand. I'm not asking for anything for myself. I want that understood, not even for him, but for the country, which is more in need than ever of people capable of pulling it out of the hole.' Antonio Pérez said, among other things, that he'd always admired my firm will, my tenacity to get ahead despite the adverse circumstances in which I found myself, my aptitude as a student, our good relationship, despite the ill-fated star that had ruled his married life, that, sadly, had ended in a humiliating disappointment on his part. He asked me if I was aware of the separation, and I played dumb, or rather surprised. What else could I do! Antonio Pérez opened his heart to me; it was obvious that at that moment he needed to open up to someone, to let all the bitterness he'd stored away for so many years escape. He displayed a generous side that I didn't expect from him. He didn't want to blame anyone. 'In a divorce,' he said, 'it's difficult to find a culprit in the strictest sense; there are no absolute victims or executioners, only two human beings who suffer and recognize their error in making a rash decision. The only thing I have any interest in telling you, and I want to be entirely frank, to speak to you as the brother you've always been to me, is that if anyone has not, I repeat, not, been guilty of the sordidness that my family life has become, it is I. You know your sister's character better than anyone else, you too have suffered from it and have been on more than one occasion its victim, so we'll not belabor it. Fortunately I can talk to you like this. You are now old enough to weigh the facts; I trust your judgment.' He reminded me of certain favors he'd done for my mother, of which I was unaware, thanked me for the fact that neither she nor I had ever interfered in their family affairs. At that point he began to talk to the Licenciado Iglesias, who worked at the Ministry of Education, about the scholarship to Italy, and he repeated the confidence he had in me and the certainty he had that I would return it. He added something about the important role that the future had in store for me, the need the country had for persons that would honor and give it prestige, et cetera, et cetera, without giving me the opportunity to utter a single word. Finally, before saying goodbye, the Licenciado Iglesias gave me his card and asked that I visit him the following week; he asked me to bring with me such and such documents. And a month later, before I knew it, I'd disembarked at the port of Genoa." De la Estrella realized that it had been a mistake to begin the story of his trip to Istanbul with that family incident. All that was left was for them to ask him about his sister and how he'd resolved the matter of the money with his brother-in-law. The classic whitewashed tombs! Perhaps they'd have been happy to return to the blackmail Blanca had devised, right down to the final details. Family unity over crime! We'll cause a scandal in the press if you don't cough up the dough! Beautiful, isn't it? "I hadn't promised Blanca anything, except to feel the interrogatee out; on listening to him, although I never much cared for him, and without his having to offer more arguments, I remembered such repugnant traits about my sister's character that I felt I couldn't go on with the performance without vomiting." De la Estrella's stare became even more glazed, his voice harsher. He'd wanted to gradually reach the moment when—to his misfortune—he met, and the circumstances in which he dealt with, that pair of siblings who ruined his trip to Istanbul and prevented him from properly admiring the Blue Mosque and the many other artistic gems the city possessed, and not only that, but also robbed him of happiness and calm for the rest of his life. Their names were Marietta and Alexander, as he'd already said, but he'd taken the wrong route, at least at the beginning. He saw those former Spanish exiles; he was sure that neither the bombings nor prisons they'd suffered could compare to the hardships he'd endured during his life, not to mention the architect and his children, for whom surely everything had been peaches and cream, grapefruit juice and hot chocolate at whatever time of the day they had the whim.

Because that's how it was; the Millares family had turned their backs on him, concentrating on their banal pursuits, as if listening to the story implied some moral commitment. If they'd only known Blanca! he thought again. If they only knew what that bitch was capable of! Out of the corner of his eye he saw that Salvador

Millares was smiling as if he were enjoying a humorous passage in the dime novel he was reading. He knew he was laughing at him. He regretted not sending him to the slammer for a couple of years when he had the chance. He deserved it for all the irregularities he'd committed; at one point he lacked the paperwork to justify certain purchases. The expenses had been paid, that was true, the purchased materials existed, he could prove it, the construction was carried out and at a lesser cost than expected, but without proper documentation. When he punished Millares, he wasn't penalizing theft but disorder. Something that on principle he couldn't accept. Who could assure him that it wasn't a clever ruse by the young architect to accustom him to treat matters so casually, to gain his trust, to keep him under his thumb, and, when he least expected it, stab him in the back, causing him to tremble for the rest of his life? He couldn't allow it. So he deducted the unsupported amounts from his salary, they tore up the contract, and afterward they had nothing to do with each other. That was all. He saw Millares's sister stop what she was doing, look at him curiously, and raise her hand. He had to prevent her from opening her mouth, to stifle any stupid questions beforehand. Without wasting a second, he explained that he'd met Rodrigo Vives in Mexico City, that they'd gone to preparatory school together; even then he was a pedantic and self-important student, a crafty little politician who shortly after entering school had become president of the Student Union, that one had gone on to study law and the other anthropology, and in the interim they'd stopped seeing each other.

"We met again in Rome, thanks, if thanks is in fact the right word, to an employee of the Consulate from whom I managed to wheedle an invitation to lunch from time to time. I must caution you that I didn't consider myself a freeloader in any way; those invitations came at a price, and I was willing to pay it, why not, which consisted of listening throughout the meal to practical lessons on elegance. He'd tell me which ties to wear, how to match their colors with suits and socks, where his shirts were made, even his underwear. Dessert and coffee were invariably devoted to shoes, a subject that enraptured him. For certain events and at certain times of the day, English footwear was preferable over Italian. That was the true proof of dressing well. Yes, the shoes had to be English, they could be Alexander or Barker, but for important occasions the only shoes that mattered were Church's. 'Don't forget,' he'd tell me. 'Go to the shoe store and ask for Church's, no other brand. Church's! It's better to buy them a size bigger than normal, because they are a bit narrow around the border of the sole. That's their *charm*,' he'd say in English. I can't say that at the time I dressed but rather I did my best to cover myself, but I listened to him patiently. He paid for my food and arranged jobs for me showing Mexicans around Rome. I also served as a guide for Vives around the city. He talked and talked and talked, and I was happy to listen to him. At that time, as a rule, I was reduced to watching and listening; I formed impressions of things and filed them away. I was, you might say, a walking databank. I hadn't earned that scholarship to commit myself willy-nilly to anything or anyone. I noticed that Vives moved about and managed much more comfortably than a normal tourist. Every day a fortune in shirts, ties, restaurants, bookstores, and shows slipped through his fingers. I, on the other hand, saved as much as I could from my scholarship, spent entire afternoons in my room or in the street instead of going to a movie or a café, and I'd even managed to earn a little extra income. It didn't take long for me to realize that although he was interested in monuments, museums, and concerts, to the point of exclaiming at every opportunity that he couldn't do without them, it was also true that women wielded no smaller attraction over him. I introduced him to a cousin of Elena's, a dry cleaner with whom I had the sweetest relationship, but neither she nor any of my friends seemed to arouse his appetite. He was a snob, as you may have gathered by now, an insecure one; it's possible that dating a waitress or a laundrywoman made him feel insignificant. 'Oh really, then to hell with him!' I said to myself, and I took him to certain places that I was able to locate with the help of a cab driver to satisfy the illustrious visitors whom I was tasked to show around and thus earn a few lire, and where apparently Vives felt very much at home."

"Be careful what you say, Doc, don't overstep the mark," Millares demanded.

"No need to worry!" he replied somewhat abashedly, although annoyed by the overfamiliar "Doc" directed at him. "Never you mind. I know the limits." And he continued: "As I said, it was Vives who spoke and I who listened; but don't think that I was a passive audience, not at all. It would have been very easy for me to tell him that his constant lectures were getting on my nerves and ruining what little good humor I had, but I preferred instead to egg him on. Speak to a fool according to his folly, as the saying goes. I wasn't a timid listener; on the contrary, truth be told I was the one who directed the conservation. I questioned him; I pretended to argue with him, but it was merely a game to allow him to shine. I left him with the idea that he'd dazzled me, that every day he was discovering new horizons in my life, that he'd gained a disciple, ready to die for his ideas. Rodrigo Vives was extremely ambitious, and I encouraged those ambitions. I swaddled him in excessive praise, without his noticing the game I was playing. If he'd had an ounce of brains, he'd have told me to piss off five times a day. Forgive me! I swear that will be the last time I use such ungilded language! It seems that I can't free myself of the concept that certain insignificant people have of a feast. Forgive me, my lady! Forgive me, o innocent infanta, for using certain words! The only thing I'm attempting to explain is that a better relationship couldn't have been established. Rodrigo had been living in Paris for three years. He was about to finish his anthropology studies, which, incidentally, in the end served no purpose. Before leaving Rome, he asked what I was planning to do that summer. I must remind you that I'm talking about the year 1961. Our meeting must have taken place at the end of May or the beginning of June. I told him that I was staying in Rome; I didn't think it would be difficult to find a job during the holiday. I added, to gain his interest, that I needed some money for books, to travel a bit. I couldn't afford not to encounter the sources of culture while in Italy; I considered it a duty to civilize myself a bit before returning to Mexico, etcetera, etcetera. I was almost sure he'd invite me to Paris. He didn't. Instead he told me that his sister Ramona would be arriving from Mexico that summer and that they were planning to travel to Turkey. He asked if I wouldn't mind joining their adventure, as his guest. 'So much the better,' I mumbled to myself, and of course I accepted. We agreed to meet on a certain day in August in Venice. We'd arrange the details by correspondence. We'd travel by train to Istanbul, on the Orient Express no less! My generation, every generation I imagine, had their own particular obsessions, their own fixations. It was all the same to me, but not to my contemporaries. It was essential to carry out certain rituals, whether one liked them or not; one of them was to travel, if only once in a lifetime, on the Orient Express. Rodrigo and Ramona would board the train in Paris, and I would join them in Venice. I've never liked to throw money around willy-nilly! My trips, I have already said that in one period of my life I had the opportunity to make several, I always made at the expense of the public treasury. I got to my room and made my calculations. From what I gathered from the conversation, Vives took it for granted that I was going to cover the trip from Rome to Venice, which seemed petty to me; but then I couldn't yet imagine the many surprises that my dealings with the exquisite project that was that nonentity and his happy sister would bring me. I wouldn't make the trip by hitchhiking as I didn't consider it safe, and, on that occasion, I intended to take my savings with me, not to spend them, of course, but because I had no place or person I could fully trust in Rome. In any case, the train to Venice wasn't expensive, although anything more than a plate of pasta at that time was already an attack on my pocket. After all, I was living from day to day, without a millionaire father like the Viveses. Apart from the scholarship, not a penny more from Mexico. My brother-in-law Antonio had vaguely alluded to a sum that he never sent. Ask my sister for help? Not in a million years! That would have exposed me to another of her insulting letters. My income from showing visitors from Mexico around Rome was sacred, untouchable; with those tips I was building my personal wealth. I don't want to dwell on the details, but suffice it to say that one fine day in August, as sure as a well-aimed arrow, I found myself on the platform of the Venice station next to the Paris-Istanbul Pullman." De la Estrella paused, as if to allow his reduced audience to savor that lavish metaphor; he stood up, walked to the picture window, remained there for a moment, contemplating the storm in perfect silence, then returned to his seat and continued: "As soon as the door opened, Rodrigo Vives exited, almost leaping. Behind him, with the air of a little rich girl, dressed like a doll, lifting a ruffly canary-yellow skirt with her dainty porcelain fingers, his sister, the

Ramoncita about whom I had been forewarned and who was to treat me to so many unpleasant moments during the next few days, glided down. At first, I thought I had met her in Mexico, but I couldn't say where or when. Perhaps it was just that she was much like every other girl of her age, that is, she lacked her own personality. A nonentity, just like the protagonist of one of the most brilliant novels of all time, ladies and gentlemen. Except, unlike that novel, instead of illuminating what she touched, she was able to darken even the most radiant spring day. It's not even worth commenting on her meager personality. A couple of minutes were enough for me to size up the famous Vives siblings: all talk, façade, feigned elegance; at the first opportunity they showed themselves to be the deadbeats they were! Rodrigo embraced me, introduced me to his sister, 'mi fratella Ramona,' and asked me in which car I was going to be sitting. I stared at him with all the perplexity in the world. 'Where am I going to sit?' I repeated mechanically, but said to myself: 'What do you mean where am I am going to sit, you little shit?' Don't you realize? He thought that I'd bought my ticket. Vives finally understood that wasn't the case. There was no time left to go to the ticket counter at the station. He began to speak in French with a train employee. He then addressed me with something that bordered on exasperation: 'The train's packed. It's August,' as if I didn't know that. 'There are only second-class seats. This man will escort you and issue you a ticket. No problem. We'll spend most of our time in the dining car. Go drop off your bag and come back so we can get something to eat.' Again I froze. I didn't like his officious tone at all, let alone the whole matter about paying for my ticket. I made a decision. I wasn't going to get into an argument in front of the clerk and Ramona about who should pay the fare. I would do it myself, and when the time was right I'd talk to

Rodrigo and ask him to return the money so his invitation would be just that, an invitation. But they'd already ruined my day. And off goes Dante de la Estrella, Esquire, on the verge of completing a doctorate in Europe, to leave his suitcase in a train car crammed with Turks and return to the five-star compartment to pay tribute to the serene highnesses! Was it fair to make someone, a supposed guest besides, feel such an affront? No, it wasn't! But it was much more unfair to allow me, me, who lived day-to-day, to pay for my own trip, when Rodrigo Vives had assured me personally and in writing that he'd take care of all the expenses. In short, allow me to omit the disappointment I suffered when I learned where I was to travel for a whole day and night, and skip ahead a couple of hours to when the three of us were sitting in the dining car. What airs, good grief! The Viveses thought themselves royalty. He considered himself the most brilliant anthropologist in the world. He was to return to Mexico to revolutionize his discipline. Ramona humored him constantly; I've never known a woman who fawned over a brother so shamelessly! He was like a god to her; that much was clear. To think that she's now a university professor! Some things truly defy explanation! I don't doubt that anyone in this ever-changing world can improve herself. I've personally witnessed amazing transformations. But there are cases where no improvement can happen. It's impossible. Because of an absence of a quorum of brain cells, quite simply. If someone told me that my wife had become an enlightened, understanding, pleasant woman, I'd reply, 'Yes, señor, thank God she has, and I'm glad you witnessed it,' but I'd be absolutely aware that there was some confusion, that I was being told about someone who was by no means my wife, or that the speaker had suddenly gone mad. There are cases, I repeat, in which change is impossible. Señorita Vives is one of them. Her mediocrity knew no bounds. We had lunch and dinner on the train. We drank superb wine. Ramona demanded that her brother's attention, and as a result mine, focus on her and her tiny world of trivialities and caprices. Ramona Vives had to finish her thesis. For I don't know what reason she wanted to graduate as soon as possible. Her problem, she said, was that all subjects were equally attractive to her. The dramatic quality of her personality, she added, was her inability to make a decision. She planned to make a list of ten or twelve topics that appealed to her and choose at random. She did nothing but call attention to herself with her whining and fawning. And that mousy voice! Good grief! What surprised me the most was that Rodrigo took her seriously. She should attempt, he recommended, a kind of literary essay that addressed the contributions of philosophical anthropology, one that followed the devil's trail, about the voluptuousness of death, shall we say, in our literature, from the chronicles of the conquistadors to the present. To study seriously Sahagún, for example, who, as soon as he disembarked, stumbled upon the ubiquitous and mutable presence of the devil in everything that New Spain offered. 'Yes, Ramona,' he'd say with facile eloquence, in one of those velvet voices that all the leading men of Mexican cinema used to seduce María Antonieta Pons. 'It has become fashionable to examine our old myths, to catalog what has survived of them, to delve into the text and probe that dark miasma that lies beneath the obvious, to scrutinize what writing gestures faintly toward and without which no literary work would exist as such.' And there, my friends, he launched into one of those little dissertations of which he was so fond; the ones I'd listened to in Rome were, by comparison, mere babble, dotted with names of French, English, and German philosophers, writers, and anthropologists, even a Romanian. Give me a goddamn break! He spoke about a political anthropology that was necessary to grasp a true discourse of power. No one, according to him, in Mexico was working on the novels of the nineteenth century and, above all, on those of the Revolution, other than their express political discourse; on the other hand, critics fail to consider the political concept that is embedded, diluted, in the narrative discourse, which appears obliquely in certain actions, appears in elements such as costumes, movements of the body, and reveals, in the end, the author's true political concept, although sometimes contrary to express statements. As he spoke about this hypothetical thesis, Rodrigo became lost in a thousand twists and turns, symbolic concepts, the sacred and the profane, the return to a clear philosophical formulation of Greek mythology, the concepts of the alchemists, etcetera, etcetera, etcetera. 'Everything else is banal, fratella of my soul,' he concluded, almost exhausted. She listened to him spellbound, without understanding, I would venture, a single thing, as if she were listening to him speak in another language. 'Tell me, what is that, Brother, what do you eat it with, how do you cook it, do you add capers or olives, do you think it would be possible to add some slices of *longaniza*,' the innocent lamb's eyes seemed to say. I took advantage of a pause to clarify that in Italian, a language I knew well by then, the word for brother is *fratello*; and that sister was *sorella*; that saying *fratella* and *fratellita mia* was total nonsense, and they responded in unison with a resounding guffaw. I became annoyed. I sulked. I made a display of looking at my wristwatch. I considered telling them that it was time for me to retire to my multifamily car. But he put his hand on my arm, as if to prevent me, and, suddenly no longer laughing, he began to tell me about his interest in going to Istanbul. He intended to visit Marietta Karapetiz, the widow of the celebrated traveler and anthropologist Aram Karapetiz, a yet-to-be-discovered classic of our century's ethnography. That was the moment I first heard her name mentioned. Never could I have imagined that it would hold such tremendous importance in my destiny. I owe to her, despite her, my initiation into literature; she was the driving force that led me to write dozens of critical articles in which, I must make clear, I made her eat dirt on more than one occasion. It was because of her that I discovered the great Nikolai Vasilyevich Gogol, whose work has illuminated even the darkest moments of my life. Rodrigo continued to prattle on the entire time until we retired to our respective cars—they to their cushioned berths, and I to sit on an excruciatingly hard wooden seat, surrounded by various bundles and smells, none of them interesting—and even during the times we met the following day in the railroad dining car, about the enthusiasm that the exotically named couple aroused in him. Marietta Karapetiz was the faithful and devoted custodian of her late husband's papers, but she wasn't content to be merely the traditional widow of such an eminent man. Vives emphasized the importance of her own work. She was a prominent Slavicist, a university professor, and author of fascinating monographs on Russian literature. Most recently she spent several months a year lecturing at American universities. Rodrigo and she had been corresponding since before he arrived in Paris, that is to say, since finding in Mexico one day, in some old history journals, Karapetiz's *Chronicle* of his travels throughout southern Mexico. He considered them to be works of the highest quality and of still-fashionable interest. A man educated in the Golden Age of anthropology! In the prime of his youth, he'd participated in an expedition to New Guinea and another to Central Asia. Later he traveled with his wife to Mexico and Central America. 'From there I learned,' the boy who'd never left an office or a library announced sententiously, 'that the real work is done where the events happen, in life, and not in laboratories and university carrels.' The Revolution had caught Karapetiz and his young wife by surprise in the jungle of Tabasco. They'd lived in our country for several years and traveled extensively. Their visit to Mexico, in light of the historical moment, passed completely unnoticed. The country wasn't conducive to such adventures. They ran into countless obstacles; at times their movements appeared suspicious, so much so that to avoid any major incident, they decided to return to Europe. Karapetiz taught in Germany and in Switzerland. Shortly before the start of the war he accepted an offer from the University of Ankara and settled in Turkey. As soon as Vives arrived in Europe, he contacted the widow. They'd met on one occasion in Paris and on another in Geneva. And he repeated over and over again the same palinode: a perfect polygraph, a humanist, a woman more at home in the Renaissance than in our withered days. 'She can speak of the clear blue of the Aegean and the cobalt of the Sea of Marmara, of the caramel dessert he savored at breakfast that morning, of the oppressive heat of the afternoons and the coolness of the high plateaus of Anatolia, of a jacket, a handbag, and the high heels she was planning to buy in the afternoon in an altogether unremarkable shop, where everything on display, which was little, was of perfect quality, and beneath her words will forever flow like burning lava the river of thought. Everything she mentions in the end alludes in some way to culture.' For the love of God! And there you have it! The frustrated promise that was the ambitious Rodrigo Vives was capable of affectation on that scale, and even greater. That river of lava did indeed flow through Señora Karapetiz's veins, but it rarely had anything to do with culture. I met her two days later. Oh, and the circumstances! I've never been so humiliated in my life! A

humanist, the famous Little Hands of Silk? A Renaissance sensibility? Sometimes she's even appeared in my dreams. There she's
called Little Hands of Shit. I wake up and still seem to hear her
whiskey-soaked voice, the grinding of her portentous teeth, her
endlessly boastful logorrhea, and I shiver. I don't associate her figure with the Muses, or her words with poetry. On the contrary, it's
a purulent river, a lava of filth that gushes from her lips. Even in my
dreams I can smell the stench of sulfur that emanated from her
mouth in real life."

Lightning flashed across the sky at that moment. A cascade of
lights and a roar that made the windowpanes tremble seemed the
natural accompaniment to the Licenciado's words. Amelia Millares
looked up from her crosheting, turned her gaze to the visitor, and
in a serious voice said:

"It seems to me, Licenciado, that you've unleashed the violent
elements. One must learn to take certain disappointments more
calmly." And she buried herself once again in her crocheting.

The storyteller seemed to come out of his trance. He looked at
the others in amazement, like a lost child trying to find his way out
of the forest. No one seemed to respond to his silent call, absorbed
as they were in their tasks. The Blue Mosque stubbornly refused
to come together. He looked resentfully at Millares; one by one,
he surveyed all the members of the family. Had he merely played
the role of a street vendor whose product no one wanted? Had he
labored in vain? He wanted to scream. Had his words been little
more than a cantilena that served as a counterpoint to the storm
raging outside to lull Millares's insipid reading and his family's man-
ual arts? Had nothing he'd said been worth listening to? To them
he didn't exist, nor did his relationship to ancient Constantinople,
whose walls he'd touched with his own hands, the ancient and

oft-desecrated capital of Byzantium, the Sublime Porte. Who did they think they were? Belonging to what privileged race? Without showing his disillusion, on the contrary, with a sharp voice and an increasingly peremptory tone, he continued:

"Sometimes I wonder, does anyone today remember Rodrigo Vives and his cosmic aspirations? Look, Millares, if there was one thing my classmates in preparatory school were sure of, it was his future glory. Even I, who am not given to growing fond of people at first sight and who always try to play devil's advocate, eager to point out mistakes and dismiss achievements, came to believe at a certain point in his brilliant future. As you all can see, he returned to Mexico and single-handedly clipped his own wings. At the joint! Don't you agree, Millares?" And because the interrogatee didn't answer but continued to read his Simenon, the Licenciado proceeded in an even more spiteful tone, shouting: "Much was expected of him, and he ended up as a mediocre bureaucrat, yes, one of many, drab, indecisive, devoid not only of lofty projects but rather a middling interest in anything. After our stay in Turkey, mine was very brief, as I have already said, our friendship was damaged forever. For years we didn't even say hello to each other. Lately I've lowered my guard, out of pity, after seeing him so defeated: Did I mention that Karapetiz departed this life? From then on, we began to speak again. We said hello, exchanged a few words on occasion, said goodbye without amity, but also without rancor. The human being's capacity for surprises is limitless. If there was an offended party in Istanbul, it was I. Ridiculed and swindled to boot. I was humiliated in the most repulsive manner. I fled, without saying goodbye, I admit, but I was right. Neither Rodrigo Vives nor the now famous Ramoncita, the now university professor, ever offered so much as an apology. From him I might have accepted it, from her not on your life. They made me pay for my round-trip tickets and the hotel. They kept my suitcase. I lost my watch, a pen, and a good part of the savings I'd managed to pull together in Rome. Over time I've come to think that Vives wasn't as malicious as I thought him to be at the time. It wasn't viciousness but rather ignorance, naïveté, that caused him to throw me into the beast's cage. His blindness to that woman's deception was genuine. Just listening to him was enough: 'You have to meet her. To listen to her is a feast. A truly brilliant woman; a mind forged in the Enlightenment and a Renaissance sensibility. It's this integration of opposites that makes her so radically contemporary.' Today such language is decidedly cartoonish, but I swear he was serious, and a pedant. In any case, he was the only one responsible for that absurd adventure. When, if not for his invitation, would it have occurred to me to travel to Turkey? And as for the invitation, as I've already explained, it turned out to be the most expensive trip I've ever taken in my life. Of course, he was primarily responsible! First, for taking me there, then for abandoning me, excusing himself on the pretext of a throat condition. All of us, ladies and gentlemen, have had a cold, a sore throat, and yet we've all accepted responsibility when necessary. Not him. Well, the past is the past, smoke, some say, my wife among them. I wish she were too! I'm not so sure; there are wounds that never heal completely. That's all I can add. Poor Vives! If you think about it, you realize that he could only come out defeated. His sycophants caused him to lose, but more than anything else his inability to touch and recognize reality. He wasn't the intellectual he thought he was. He wasn't the teacher of America, nor the public figure his peers expected. Don't you agree, Millares?"

The architect made vague gestures of exasperation, sketched some vague movement with his hands that committed him to nothing. He'd never met Rodrigo Vives, had never even heard his name, and couldn't imagine what hopes his subsequent failure had dashed. He didn't know, nor did he care. It was evident that as long as that buffoon remained in his house, it was going to be difficult for him to continue his novel. He closed the book, looked toward the window; the downpour continued. He poured himself another glass of brandy, leaned back in his chair, and sullenly contemplated the storm.

III

Wherein the author relates the arrival of three Mexicans to Istanbul, and how from the first moment the imminent appearance of the controversial Señora Karapetiz is augured.

"WE MUST HAVE ARRIVED IN the Turkish capital very early in the morning," De la Estrella continued, "although not too early because we still had time to have breakfast on the train. The first thing we did, it goes without saying, was to head to the hotel to drop off our bags. We had rooms reserved at the Pera Palace, one of those vaguely legendary hotels that had managed to survive the century's collectivization of tourism. I went up to my room and stayed there only as long as necessary. I shaved and took a shower; I didn't do anything else. I went down to the ground floor, where Ramona was already waiting for me. Something in her gaze caused me to sense a hint of disapproval that I found quite impertinent, the kind of unspoken accusations that can be more vexing than an open reproach, confirmed immediately by the unfriendly tone with which she underscored that I'd taken more than a century to come down, insinuating that in that time she and her brother had dealt with a thousand matters of capital importance. Yes, indeed, while I frivolously squandered away my life in my ablutions! She told me that Rodrigo had informed Professor Karapetiz that we'd arrived, or, rather, confirmed it to her, as he'd already telegrammed her from Paris the means, day, and time of our arrival. 'With those details,' I remarked, as if in passing, 'the proper thing would have been to wait for us at the station, or at least send someone to help us retrieve our bags from that mayhem, don't you think?' Then, with a knowing tone, as if there were something unseemly about the relationship, I asked her, 'By the way, how old is this distinguished woman whose absence causes your brother to feel so anxious?' 'I don't know,' she replied rather bewildered. 'Rodrigo has always been like that. As far back as I can remember, he's been just as he is now, orderly, prompt, and efficient. As soon as he arrives somewhere, he outlines a program and organizes it without hesitation; he's not a man, I assure you, to get lost in trifles.' She said those words with such solemnity that for a moment I thought she was reciting a civic creed; then, in a more normal voice and attitude, she added: 'Tonight we're having dinner with her, with the Professor. I imagine you won't want to miss the opportunity. I'm almost certain that Rodrigo was planning to invite you. By the way, he should be coming down at any moment.' She paused again briefly; then, as to avoid, if still necessary, any equivocation, but with the angelic condescension belonging to one explaining something to a mindless servant, she added: 'Professor Karapetiz must be an older woman. She lived in Mexico during the Revolution. Just imagine! The things you come up with! Better an old man's darling than a young man's slave, as the old saying goes, and I am of the opinion that it's preferable to clarify things from the beginning to avoid unpleasant misunderstandings later on. I know Rodrigo better than anyone else . . .' *Better than I in certain regards, those that one prefers to keep from the family, rest assured,* I was about to blurt out. I was tempted to tell her about her brother's unholy adventures

in Rome, but I restrained myself. I began that day, just like the previous one, in a foul mood. But I didn't say a word, nothing; instead,
I began to leaf through some old newspapers that were on a table
and to peruse some tourist brochures of the city. Half an hour went
by, an hour, then an hour and a half; every now and then I paced
impatiently through the lobby, looked out the door, ventured a few
steps down the street. Very prompt, my friend Rodrigo, for a talk
with his Turkish woman, very orderly, yes señor, very efficient in
organizing his affairs, but to hell with the rest of us! When I saw
that the morning was slipping away and he still hadn't appeared, I
went back to Ramona, who was sitting in a lounge chair reading a
big blue guidebook and taking some notes, and I chided her: 'Do
you think he's still talking to his Turkish woman? Don't you think
he's gone too far?' Trying to talk to Ramona was a task I envy no
one. You had to see her: a spoiled little girl with no imagination,
no social graces, despite coming from an environment where you'd
think such things are taken for granted. I'd ask her a question and
she'd say yes or no, then become quiet again. I'd ask her another
question after a while, and she'd answer the same way: yes, no,
maybe, who knows, hopefully, without the slightest interest in having a conversation. After fifteen minutes of dealing with her, even
the calmest man would have sunk into despair. Imagine what it was
like to be alone with her for an hour and a half that seemed as if
it would never end! I tried calling Rodrigo several times, but his
phone was always busy. Several times I asked Ramona to go upstairs
and get her brother. She refused. Nothing bothered Rodrigo more,
she recited, than being rushed. He was an expert at organizing his
time. 'I can see that!' I told her, fuming. And as if she didn't hear
me, she repeated again that Rodrigo was very orderly, very prompt,
and very efficient. I couldn't contain myself any longer. 'Look, my

dear,' I said, 'he'll show up when it suits him, no sooner. You and I are sitting here like a pair of oxen, wasting precious time. I would have preferred to spend more time in the bathroom or stay in bed for another hour, which I could use; allow me to remind you that I didn't sleep in a comfy berth but on a hard wooden seat. At the rate we're going, we won't even see the city today. Something tells me that your brother won't be ready until tonight when we go out to celebrate our nuptials with Sofia.'"

"With whom?" asked Amelia Millares, interested at last, it seemed, in the story.

"Ramona asked me the same question, and I now offer the same answer to you. With wisdom! That's what Sofia means. From the Greek *sophos:* to know, knowledge, understanding of something. I'd heard that expression from a professor in Rome, and I'd bring it out from time to time, almost always to very good effect. I was referring to that Turkish woman, who, according to Rodrigo Vives, contained in herself the entire knowledge of the Universe. I was more than fed up, but you must understand, I was a guest; out of dignity, principle, and politeness, I didn't want to go looking for Rodrigo. I ran the risk that the next day he'd send me to buy him cigarettes, or bring him coffee, even towels to his room. So I asked a bellhop to go up to Rodrigo's room and tell him that we'd been waiting for him all morning, and also to ask him if he planned to stay at the hotel for the rest of the day, so we'd know what to expect. Instead of the bellhop, Vives himself came down. He gave me excuses, albeit dismissively, again like a servant. He'd fallen asleep with the phone in his hand while trying to call my room. 'Over an hour!' he exclaimed. 'An hour and a half, to be precise.' 'Who would think!' He seemed amazed at his own delay. He said he felt ill, feverish; his joints and throat were hurting. Indeed, he looked terrible. He took a couple of aspirin and a strong coffee, and we left the hotel. And so, with a very poor physical disposition on his part and a rather sour mood on mine, our first walk through the city began."

"Listen, are you ever going to tell us what happened in Istanbul? Why all this rigmarole and reluctance? I think I'm finally getting it. At the beginning the sister gave you a reason to think she was interested, but as the trip went on she changed her mind. Is that right?"

That observation from the old man Millares, until that moment so quiet, focused on arranging his cards in long rows and moving them with an exasperating lack of urgency, only to come out with such a doddering remark, was about to unhinge the visitor. He restrained himself as best he could so as not to respond with a hurtful phrase that might lead the old man's son to throw him out onto the street in the middle of the storm. He must acknowledge that even now it's hard for him to admit to himself that from the moment Vives told him that his sister would be accompanying them on the trip to Turkey he'd concocted certain vain illusions. Perhaps a tender feeling had been born when they met. Perhaps on a not-so-distant day he too could slip his feet into a shiny new pair of Church's shoes, like Rodrigo and the employee at the Consulate in Rome, disregard the fears that the future held for him, own a home in Piedras Negras, or in the capital, and even on the beach; he deserved it, why not? It wouldn't be a bad idea to give it a try, but a certain contemptuous attitude shown by Ramona on the train and, above all, her behavior that morning discouraged him. He wasn't in the mood to put up with the fussiness, whims, and gratuitous braying of a Little Miss Know-It-All. He preferred to ignore Millares's father's words, and he continued his speech:

"Not so much has happened in my story, my dear good man, that you should already be growing impatient. On the contrary, the opposite could be said about that morning. A grave lack of activity. Rest assured, there will be action, enough to provide a glimpse into some of the most extravagant aberrations the human species is capable of conceiving. The initial plan was to stay a week in Istanbul, and from there continue on to Ankara and perhaps Smyrna. It's possible that the Viveses did so. I never knew. I escaped the next day. My escape, I would like to clarify, wasn't that of a criminal, but rather of a respectable man terrified, or at least disturbed, by any manifestation of madness. I cannot boast of being an expert on that city, I didn't assimilate it. If I were asked: 'Dante, can you be our guide in Constantinople?' I would have to decline out of professional honesty, no matter how much I was offered. My experience was of a different kind: a dizzying journey into the depths of myself, for which that colorful and bustling city served only as a setting. In short, it was very late that day when we finally began our itinerary. A quick, superficial, if I may say, insignificant visit to the heart of the city of mysteries; we walked through the bewildering swarm of the Grand Bazaar, had lunch in a restaurant along the way, which must have cost a pittance, and a couple of hours of rest in our hotel to recharge, which was the best part of the morning. We were all exhausted, restless, irritated. The end of the festivities would take place in the evening. We would take a tour along the Bosporus Strait to the Sea of Marmara; then: the great moment, the much-ballyhooed appearance of Marietta Karapetiz. Oh, our leader never failed to repeat throughout the day the many virtues of that extraordinary woman! In the restaurant, in the bazaar, on the street, we heard her curriculum vitae: the widow of a famous ethnographer whose work she covetously preserved, a woman of letters who had excelled on her own merits, etcetera, etcetera, etcetera. However, he willfully withheld from us one or two things. He was saving the truth for later, in case I was unable to discover it on my own. So was the real Vives!"

"Well, Doc, that sounds rather promising! That little gem must have been worth a fortune. I imagine you must have enjoyed meeting her." This time it was the architect himself who interrupted.

De la Estrella shuddered. He didn't like the overfamiliar "Doc," which had been hurled at him for the second time that afternoon. But, in any case, in those words, which sounded to him like cheap comedy, he'd perceived a certain interest from his former partner, thinly veiled in sarcasm. He remained silent for a few minutes, as if stunned under the titanic weight of memory, then, in a voice that suddenly ceased to be shrill and hysterical and acquired a certain dignified baritone, he said deliberately:

"I'm not a man of easy confidences, Millares. Quite the contrary. I want to put on the record that this is the first time I've spoken about my trip. Not even my wife knows in detail the circumstances surrounding it. I'd have to be mad to share them with her! More than a quarter of a century has passed. I was very young then; I knew little or nothing about the world, even though my previous life had always been difficult, and I'd had to overcome very thorny situations to get ahead. However, that adventure was so intense that I was on the verge of losing my self-respect forever. I had my talents, naturally, thanks to which I'd managed to survive, to complete a law degree, but, deep down, I swear, a more innocent, wholesome boy could scarcely be found in this world. I was a romantic. For me a woman was the equivalent of a goddess. To find myself suddenly mixed up with that rabble! What conversations, my God, what manners!" De la Estrella began to wave his hands in front of his eyes, as if trying to erase certain visions. "Especially the next day, at the home of that monument to wisdom where I ended up, when I *naïvely* believed I was already his friend and was struggling to cement that friendship that, victim of a sudden bout of senility, seemed at that moment the only important cause worth giving my life for. I'm getting ahead of myself, I know, forgive me, I'm zigzagging all around; speaking isn't easy for me, not easy at all. I was commenting on the first outing, wasn't I? And our return to the hotel. I hadn't yet met Marietta Karapetiz or her brother Alexander, or Sacha, or whatever you want to call him, and here I am skipping to the afternoon of the next day, when I arrived at her home and the aforementioned little brother, with no clothes on his body other than a white robe, took me by the arm, pulled me away from the others, and, dragging his crippled leg, forced me to follow him to the balcony, where he blurted out the following speech: 'Be patient, my friend! You're young, and, as such, you take pleasure in tormenting her,' he heaved a monumental sigh, as if he had a large bellows between his chest and back, and continued, 'My poor sister! You can't imagine what she's gone through in this dirty life!' I began to mumble meaningless words, out of surprise. I tried to tell him that bothering or tormenting her was the farthest thing from my mind, that, on the contrary, I endeavored to offer her my friendship. I wanted to make him understand that Ramona wasn't the only person here worthy of his friendship; to warn him about the duplicity of that fraudster, to show him that she didn't deserve his affection, that she was scheming with all her might to separate us. I told him that he'd soon see how different reality was from what he believed. That if he paid attention, he'd realize that I longed to make Marietta know that my heart, albeit somewhat wounded by her sarcasm, belonged to her; but without listening, without paying the slightest attention to what I'd said, he continued to sing the same old song: 'No one can imagine what my poor sister has suffered! Just look at her! With such a strong, flexible body, with her grace and long legs, she could've been the queen of belly dancers. A star, I assure you! Imagine Leda dancing before a rapt Swan! Europa, provoking the bull's lust! What sensuality, what poetry, what elegance she's able to communicate with each movement! Hers could have been a beautiful belly, like a cherub, my young friend, a seraphic belly, if not for the slash that runs from side to side, a rather fanciful scar, I wouldn't say repulsive, because it's not, don't misunderstand me, nothing of the kind. It's a wound that even possesses a strange elegance, with pink edges open in the center, where the scar becomes wider and forms a sort of tiny vulva. Oh, my friend, if you saw it, a delight, a little pink pussy, a *bocatto di cardinale*! Marietta is such an ingenious little girl that she's learned to make some belly movements with which she's able to paralyze all the muscles of her abdomen, except for the perverse lips in the center of the wound. The little mouth seems to open, close, yawn . . . There's no point in describing it to you; you'd have to see it! There are moments when I even believe that it's about to meow, that it's going to say *mamá* and *papá*.' I saw him lick his lips with an entrancing perversity. 'My sister's art,' he continued, 'you must know, is only for the elite, an ivory tower spectacle, far removed from the uncouth taste of the masses. But, my friend, you have no idea what it means to dance for that select audience. It has risks so great that she's wise not to take them'; as he said that he looked at his gammy leg with melancholy, while he affectionately patted his dead muscle in a kind of reverie. I was transfixed. I was struck with a kind of altitude sickness, vertigo. Into what had I fallen? Into what dark jungle? Was that old codger mocking me? Was he serious? I wouldn't know until the moment I was thrown into the swamp." Dante de la Estrella paused; then, with a modesty he'd not shown all the while, he murmured: "I've talked too much . . ." The pallor of his face, bathed in sweat, was frightening. In a defeated, plaintive voice, he concluded: "Yes, I've talked too much. I think you're beginning to guess . . . Anyway . . . Has the time come to reveal truths? If yes, so be it! I couldn't remain quiet any longer. In this life I've been too, too . . ." He became startled. Then, with an almost ear-piercing cry, he concluded, "Yes, I'll talk . . . ! If they must kill me tomorrow . . . !"

". . . let them kill me once and for all," Juan Ramón Millares replied jubilantly.

Licenciado De la Estrella got up from his seat, walked like an automaton to the table where the boy and his sister were putting together the puzzles. He looked at them curiously, as if rediscovering their existence. Then he smiled appreciatively. The twins had almost stopped busying themselves with the puzzles to listen to him.

"Bless you!" he murmured. His glassy eyes seemed to moisten suddenly. To hide his emotion and restore tranquility, he raised the engraving that Juan Ramón was using as a model and held it in front of his eyes. "The Blue Mosque!" he exclaimed soon after, with unnecessary emphasis, and in the same tone, without interruption, he reeled off a string of words: "Saint Sophia! Hagia Sophia, as they call it, the Golden Horn! The Grand Bazaar! The Egyptian Bazaar! The Spice Bazaar! The Pera Palace! Hagia Irene! All that is Istanbul!"

"And the Topkapi!" added Elenita.

"And the Topkapi, indeed! Of course, my dear, the Topkapi too, and three or four other little things, a couple of them abominable.

A pair of indecent siblings, carrion! Waste from the great book of Nature, masseurs! That pair too, that along with the Topkapi too, you're right, not to be forgotten, is Istanbul."

"... the Sublime Porte, ancient Constantinople, the fabled capital of Byzantium, and later of the Holy Roman Empire of the East." Juan Ramón read the text written on the back of the engraving that Dante de la Estrella had put back on the table. "Gateway that connects Europe with Asia, bridge between East and West."

"That's right, that's exactly right, thank you very much," said the visitor. "So it is, so it was, and so it shall be. No need to say more. I visited only the Bazaar, a couple of restaurants, one of them located on the shores of the Sea of Marmara, next to the mouth of the Bosporus Strait. I made a whirlwind tour of the city, a transit from nowhere to nowhere. Mere images glimpsed from the window of a rental car! A minaret here and there, and beside them the indispensable mosques. One of them, of course, must have been the Blue one, since, if not for the photographs I've studied over the years, I'd remember very little about it, as well as of the rest of that extravagant city, apart from the large crowd wandering the streets, squares, and bazaars; people of every sort and every age at all hours; some selling, some begging, others engaged in some kind of barter; women in veils and niqabs; and at all hours an ear-deafening din. All the tones that the human voice is capable of making, from the faintest whisper to the most piercing shriek, came together there. Wails, cries, petitions, sobs, murmurs shrouded and heightened by uninterrupted waves of Oriental music magnified by a chain of strategically placed loudspeakers. Three days after locking myself in my room, once back in Rome, with a fever that must have been the result of nerves, I was still unable to rid my ears of that persistent assault. My trip, I don't know if I've already mentioned, was more than anything else a journey inward, an inquiry into human evil and, at the same time, of this I can be proud, a discovery of my resistance to evil. I was crucified, dead, and buried; I descended into hell; I came to know one of its circles; I don't know if the darkest, or the most heinous, but I can attest, the most pestilent."

He suddenly noticed the look of brewing anxiety that Amelia gave Salvador Millares. He should wander off topic, he said to himself. The time had not yet come to discomfit the audience, to subjugate and confuse them. He hurried to dispel the uneasiness that his words were beginning to sow in the home.

"You may be asking yourselves: Is it really necessary that Licenciado Dante de la Estrella grace us, or more precisely inflict us, with this litany of grievances? Unfortunately, I must answer yes, such an introduction is necessary. When I say that I was in the capital of Turkey without discovering more than a fraction of its rich cultural heritage, that I didn't see its museums, nor its blue or yellow mosques, nor did I enrich my spirit in the contemplation of its masterpieces, I am obliged to point out that the circumstances weren't ideal, that certain interests were set in motion to prevent me from doing so. I know very well that I'm not before a court, but if I were, it wouldn't matter. I've never tolerated being held accountable. There was much more to see, I admit it, I recognize it, oh well! There are cities I could describe stone by stone, places of much greater transcendence in the cultural history of the world. I could spend whole days joyfully discoursing on Rome. I know Paris, London, Madrid, Seville. I've been to Houston and San Antonio several times. One day I embarked for Leningrad, the Paris of the North, that city where the illustrious Gogol lived and about which he wrote so much, so that I could walk, like Lieutenant Pirogov, from one end of Nevsky Prospekt to the other and look out over the Fontanka Canal, where that mad creature, Major Kovalyov's nose, decided to slip away. But what's the use of talking about those places? I didn't study at two universities to spend my life describing cities! It would be better to return to the days I spent in Istanbul. I've already commented on the itinerary of the first day. The second day was very different. I spent most of the morning in bed. Not without good reason. The long train ride, the slog of the previous day, the colossal lack of sleep, the dinner with Madame Karapetiz, the beastly amount of alcohol I consumed, the tobacco, the return to the hotel almost at dawn, all that left me frazzled. If I'm not mistaken, we were the last ones to leave the restaurant. While on the stairs of the restaurant, on our way out, the gypsy orchestra caught up with us, and its musicians played and sang 'Ramona' again for the ladies, who waved their arms rhythmically above their heads, while their bodies trembled like brood hens. If I allowed myself such a night today, I simply wouldn't wake up alive; I'd curl up and die in the car on the way back, or they'd find me the next day in the hotel bed in articulo mortis. My troubled soul would bid farewell forever to my mortal body. Youth is altogether something else! I was young then, and yet . . ."

"So you danced until the wee hours of the morning?" old Millares cut him off. "To tell the truth, Licenciado, you have such a way of telling things that a person seems to be learning everything, and at a certain point they realize they haven't really understood anything. Well, yes, I've caught on to something. Cupid showed up, didn't he? He shot his arrow, and the young Dante de la Estrella, Esquire. was struck clean through the heart, felled by love for your friend's sister. Why don't you tell us that you won over the old girl?"

"An old hen makes good broth!" exclaimed Amelia.

"My friend's sister, I've said and repeated several times, is named Ramona," De la Estrella affirmed in a mechanical, categorical way, trying to place himself at the margin of those vulgar characterizations, to isolate them, so they wouldn't take hold; at that moment he noticed that his memories weren't as faithful as he imagined, that at times they possessed a hallucinating clarity only to, immediately afterward, collapse and disappear into black holes. He saw with precision a thousand details, as if the events had just occurred, let's say, at the end of the previous week. He remembered the black dress Marietta Karapetiz wore in the restaurant, for example, and the excessive number of rings she wore, her long, young fingers that were never without a cigarette. He remembers the timbre of Ramona Vives's voice, her frail, girlish accent, but he's missing something essential, the emotional tapestry woven at the beginning of their relationship. He notices that when he talks about her, he tends to belittle everything about her, which he is right to do, of course, but he fears that this wasn't always the case. Would he have continued to think about Church's shoes even after meeting her? And cashmere coats and silk ties? The usual! Every time he attempts to decode the signals of his own heart, he stumbles upon an inconceivable mystery. It occurs to him that there are things that didn't happen as he's telling them, that, on the contrary, the first impression he had of Ramona Vives was that of a pretty, discreet girl, interested in a thousand nice things, happy to make this trip and anxious to enjoy it thoroughly. It was later, as the relationship evolved, that he grew to dislike her more and more, to the point of utter hatred. He remembers that when on the train she was talking about her thesis and her uncertainty in the choice of the topic, he even offered her some help that now he can't even specify. Perhaps he began to read anthropology books with her;

he doesn't really know. Rodrigo had on that occasion wrested the floor away from them to mention that thanks to her stay in Mexico, Karapetiz would have been able to understand some of the Russian authors he was studying in a new and certainly appropriate light, a concept that he'd interpreted over the years in a very different way, concluding that everything that Vives had said in his life was absolute poppycock. That intrusion prevented him from finding a more meaningful way to help the young Ramona. For Vives, the conversation on the train about his sister's thesis had been nothing more than a pretext to show off and make his way to the only subject that really interested him: the dazzling personality of Marietta Karapetiz. He had corresponded with her since she was in Mexico, and they'd met personally in Paris, in Geneva; they'd intensified their correspondence, and she'd promised to make available to him the old man Karapetiz's papers on their stay in Mexico, under the sole condition that they not leave Istanbul, that is, that he must go and read them at her home. De la Estrella thought that if Vives invited him in Rome to make the trip, he knew that Ramona would be going along, and he needed someone to take care of her, to go on walks with her, to take her out dancing, to change her diapers when she went pee-pee, while he and Karapetiz would talk for hours on end, watching the moon shimmer over the Golden Horn, read one or two yellowed documents, and, I have no doubt, have a little celebration under the pretext of recreating the myths studied by Aram Karapetiz in Mexico. He didn't succeed. Needless to say, after De la Estrella escaped, Rodrigo had to drag her along everywhere.

"You still haven't answered my question, Licenciado," said Antonio Millares.

Dante de la Estrella chose to ignore him olympianly.

"A case of pure fanaticism! Even in the evening, when I went to say goodbye, before going to dinner, Vives, with a voice that with each passing minute grew more parched, hoarse, and stifled, began to enumerate again the virtues of his favorite woman of letters, a whole series of new achievements, prestige, qualities, began to emerge, to proliferate like mushrooms in an oak grove after a rainstorm, to swell and grow with such disproportion that we ran the risk of being crushed by so many risible qualities. With each new achievement I heard, my indifference grew and transformed into distaste, annoyance, and repulsion. I was on the verge of not going to dinner, of feigning an illness. Why was Rodrigo allowed to have a sore throat, while I, who'd had a shitty day and hadn't exactly slept at the Waldorf Astoria, had to fill in for him during his engagements? Look, Millares, over time one can understand Rodrigo Vives's professional failure, his mediocre career, his personal insignificance when one remembers the disastrous way he managed his affairs. Consider, for example, the exquisite tact, the delicacy of spirit of that porcupine! God help us! He could have told me about his quills!"

De la Estrella walked to the window, made sure that it was securely fastened, that no draft was filtering in. He then turned and walked in military step to the liquor cabinet and made himself a strong whiskey soda. He alluded with extreme glibness to his ability to resist any advertising campaign that endorsed any particular product. No one knew what he was talking about any longer. Only later did it become clear that he'd not changed the subject, that he was still the victim of the obsession that had been tormenting him since the beginning of the storm.

"That's how I am!" he exclaimed triumphantly. "That's what I've become! More and more demanding, in food, in construction, in my dress, in everything. I don't let them sell me anything without first verifying its virtues. I close myself up, I shield myself, I cover myself with spines until I become a porcupine, or I retreat into my shell like a wise and wary turtle whom the years have taught much. I come more than equipped to any encounter. And it's not that I have an intransigent mind, I assure you. I try to defend myself from prejudices as well as from novelties. I'm willing to recognize the merits of others, in the same way that I admit and recognize my mistakes. If I've made a mistake in judging someone's personality, you'll always find me ready to offer my apology, to change my mind, even to kiss hands and feet when necessary. But to get to that point, the opposing side, shall we say, must have convinced me. Ramona listened entranced to her brother, already defeated, prepared for unconditional surrender, with a rapt expression in her cowlike eyes, her mouth agape, drooling. She seemed to beg to be branded with a mark that would distinguish her as an animal that belonged to such and such herd, that of Rodrigo Vives, that of Marietta Karapetiz, even that of Sacha, which would be the last straw. My case was quite different. I was, and still am, made of a different substance. I saw her revel in her brother's voice as it grew more and more extinguished, less and less intelligible, submerged in a rapturous bliss faced with the certainty that during the course of the evening, within a matter of minutes, she was to meet the wonder who was attempting to impose herself on us at all costs. But I must return to the point where I left off. After our unexceptional lunch and depressing walk that morning, we returned to the hotel. By that time I was crawling along. The three of us were moving around like the walking dead. I made it as best I could to my room and collapsed on the bed. I think I began to snore before my head hit the pillow. I must have remained in that pleasurable and welcome catatonic state for around three hours. I could have slept longer, surrendered to that deep, sound, seamless sleep until the next morning. To my dismay, I was awakened by the phone. I heard a voice that insisted on gradually pulling me out of sleep. At first I didn't understand where I was, whose voice it was, let alone what it was trying to tell me. I didn't even know if I was in Rome or in Mexico City. I ran my hand over the bed, trying to recognize it by touch, with very little result. Finally, the insistence of the voice, its tone of urgency, slowly caused the light to turn on in my brain. It was Ramoncita, who told me that Rodrigo was feeling very ill. He was burning up with fever. His throat had almost completely closed. They'd called the hotel doctor, who diagnosed a severe case of pharyngitis. An infection, pustules, and so on. He'd just given him an injection to bring down the fever. A nurse would administer more every five hours. He wasn't allowed to leave the hotel, not even the room. I thought I saw the heavens open. I said, as is customary in such cases, that I was very sorry. I offered, out of mere courtesy, my services. Could I help in any way? Go buy medicines? Anything else? I was at his disposal for whatever he needed. I wished him a speedy recovery, but with healthy dose of selfishness I was glad that I didn't have to go out that night and could instead rest properly, recover from the fatigue caused by the journey, which I hadn't yet overcome. After all, we had several days ahead of us of visits and social engagements. The important thing was for Rodrigo to get back on his feet as soon as possible. There was an ominous silence on the phone. Then mumbling, hiccups, incoherent sounds, moans began to trickle out of the receiver. What music was that? With great effort I was able to piece together and interpret those signals with which Ramona was trying to communicate with me. She explained that she'd called Professor Karapetiz to apologize, and that someone had answered with whom, due to issues of language, she was unable to make herself understood. She wasn't deterred by the difficulties with which fate was testing her and had a member of management redial the number and ask for the Professor to be called to the phone. The employee translated as he was spoken to. Neither the Professor nor her brother was at home. They had gone downtown and would arrive later . . . much . . . Much what? Ramona wanted to know, and the employee translated, and the answer wasn't long in coming. Much later, what else could it be? Both she and Señor Alexander would arrive just in time to go to bed. They'd gone downtown and would then have dinner out with some foreign friends. 'Those friends are us, don't you understand?' I replied that it wasn't at all difficult to understand. 'That's why, Dante, I'm calling you.' And with that the dreaded thrust of the knife! 'I want to ask you to go with me to the restaurant. Rodrigo is mortified beyond belief. This setback has made it even worse. Can you imagine how inconceivably discourteous it would be to stand up Professor Karapetiz in a restaurant that, to make matters worse, is on the outskirts of the city? Rodrigo has asked me to go. To offer his apologies and explain what happened. The doctor says that, if he takes care of himself, the day after tomorrow he should be completely recovered . . . His throat must . . .' I stopped her at all costs from detailing the clinical picture. Any description that has anything to do with the putrefaction of the human organism bores me to tears. Just to shut her up, I told her that she could count on me, to tell me what time we'd need to leave the hotel, that I would be ready at the time she indicated. At eight o'clock at night? All right, I would be on the first floor ten minutes before that time. I had enough time to shower and dress. I didn't wear a tie. I dressed rather casually. It was summer! August, no less! It was hellishly hot.

Ramona herself had told me on the phone that it was a restaurant on the outskirts of the city. So I put on a pair of drill pants and a sport shirt of the same material. If people in Rome, an exacting city—the Eternal City, no less!—dressed like that for dinner in summer, I didn't see why I couldn't do so in Istanbul, which for me was, and still is, the asshole of the world." A mouselike laugh could be heard in the room, but the narrator ignored it and continued. "One of Ramona's indisputable qualities was her punctuality, perhaps the only one I knew. When I got out of the elevator, she was already waiting for me in the lobby. What pretension! What affectation! What bad taste! I swear my judgment is free of any bad faith. Her dress was a blazing orange silk with a sort of pearl-green shawl of very fine thread. It was something indeed. The Viveses, for all their pretensions as San Luis Potosí aristocrats, hadn't quite made it out of the tropics. I didn't tell her what I thought; on the contrary, I commented with great affection that she looked very nice, that all she needed were some pineapples, bananas, and a few bobbles on her head to be Carmen Miranda. She replied that I might be witty, but I should forgive her for not sharing my sense of humor. We'd arranged to be at the restaurant at half past eight. We were told that we'd make the trip in half an hour at the most. We said goodbye to Rodrigo, who belabored us with the speech I've already mentioned about the exceeding moral character of the little woman we were about to meet. We wished him good night and left, and just in time, because, despite looking like a dying man, he hadn't lost his logorrhea, and you already know what his only topic was. It's possible that if I'd stayed a few more minutes, I'd have decided to decline the visit and send Ramona alone. I didn't. And I still regret it today. In theory, we had plenty of time, we would show a British sense of punctuality. But we didn't count on the difficulties we faced in getting a cab. Nor the one that came later: locating the restaurant. I don't want to bore you with our contretemps; suffice it to say that when we finally reached the restaurant, it was almost ten o'clock at night."

The Licenciado downed a shot of whiskey, which he'd poured himself a while before but hadn't touched during his delivery of the previous ill-humored soliloquy. He looked dumbfounded as he sipped his drink, as if it were a potion he was ingesting for the first time, the taste of which surprised and repulsed him in the extreme. He staggered to the sofa, with the glass still in hand, collapsed in the center, and there, without stopping, began to swig large gulps, smacking his lips, whimpering, until the large glass was empty. The effect achieved by this performance was almost greater than any other during the course of his story.

The telephone rang. The ring startled almost everyone present. Millares answered. From the dialogue that followed, it was clear that Julia, his wife, would be late, not to expect her for dinner. Millares took the opportunity to tell her that Licenciado De la Estrella was there, waiting for her, to finalize the details of a job. She burst out laughing. Was it possible that the imbecile believed that she or her mother would accept his request? She was at a loss as to how he couldn't understand; they'd been perfectly clear. She asked her husband to kick him out of the house unceremoniously. Then she changed the subject. She mentioned some new videos she was going to bring home. Something by the early René Clair, and *Dinner at Eight*, which they'd sought for quite some time, and *China Seas*, and two German films with Conrad Veidt, which were a true rarity. No, in Coyoacán it hadn't rained too much. Anyway, they'd talk later.

Millares looked at the Licenciado and thought it not the right time to pass along his wife's message. He saw a face of dejection and fury, of resignation and madness. It would be best to leave him alone, to let the crisis pass.

And at that moment the window shook again. Light invaded everything. Then the thunder clapped. The whole house shook; the windows rattled. The electricity went off for an instant. When it returned, Millares saw that the appearance of his uninvited guest was unchanged. He had merely added an expression to his face, a contemptuous smile that could just as easily have been a grimace of dread.

IV

Wherein the much-ballyhooed Marietta Karapetiz at long last appears, and her charms, which Dante C. de la Estrella does not in every moment appreciate, are revealed.

THERE WAS A PAUSE. IT could not be said that the members of the Millares family had until that moment followed Dante de la Estrella's account with equal attention. Each of them had only been interested in a few isolated moments of the story. In general, they considered the Licenciado's speech to be a permanent counterpoint to the noise caused by the rain battering the windows. Somewhat like listening to the radio. The sound was there, but no one felt compelled to give it their full attention. That familial audience, at first passive, had shifted from boredom to impatience, until, as the storyteller's muddled gibberish transformed little by little into an unstoppable force, he'd succeeded in trapping them. In the end, everyone seemed to be more or less aware of the spectacle offered by that impatient, nervous, at times almost frenzied mount, which, they were sure, would end up carrying its rider toward an unavoidable precipice. Millares had closed the novel by Simenon, resigned to learn the solution to its enigmas only after the departure of his former client. His father interrupted his hand of solitaire, and his sister Amelia paid less attention perhaps to her crocheting.

Even the twins seemed unconcerned about continuing to build the Taj Mahal and the Blue Mosque. When the Licenciado fell silent, the only noise that could be heard was the monotonous patter of rain on the windows. All eyes were focused on that homunculus with the crazed look and the almost contorted face who remained motionless in the middle of the sofa. They were looking at him, evidently awaiting clarification. No one could boast of having fully grasped the meaning of that overly excited harangue: a visit to Turkey, which for some reason had gone awry, like so many trips that are taken with others and suddenly, at the least expected moment, reveal unexpected incompatibilities, capable of destroying friendships, courtships, affairs, business partnerships. Listening to De la Estrella, one was left with the impression that the trip had turned out much worse than most, without knowing exactly why. The details offered by the narrator were rather incoherent, unless the reason for the fiasco existed in the very beginning of the account, to which no one had paid much attention. The fact that he'd purchased a train ticket didn't seem like a sufficient reason for so much excitement and such incoherent palavering.

Salvador Millares began to rejoice at the transformation suffered by that beast of prey at whose hands he'd suffered years before, the man of steel who was the source of so many terrible moments during their brief professional relationship, converted, suddenly—for what reason? the years? the electrical storm? some progressive nervous disorder?—into a glob of demoralized Jell-O, a trembling oyster that retreated from the drops of lemon falling on him. There lay the Licenciado, sniveling, shivering, frail in the middle of the sofa. He looked as if he'd given up on the story, and would remain there, transfixed in an inexplicable tantrum, until his car came to pick him up.

Amelia got up. She went to the kitchen to ask the maid to serve the coffee and refreshments she'd requested a while before. When she returned to the living room, the atmosphere was still mired. No one had returned to their previous activities. It seemed as if the very air were paralyzed, waiting for the visitor to resume the story about his trip to Istanbul. What had happened to Ramona and Rodrigo Vives? Why, above all, did he not reveal the mystery to which he seemed to allude every time he mentioned the professor with the slashed belly and such a strange name, this Marietta, whose appearance, referred to so many times, had been kept from them just when something was about to take place?

The stunned expression frozen on the Licenciado's face made it difficult to venture any comment, to risk any question. It was a respite for everyone when Amelia Millares returned to the living room from the kitchen and spoke with absolute casualness.

"The maid will serve coffee in a moment. We could all use it right about now. My husband used to say that on rainy afternoons there's nothing like a good cup of coffee, a snifter of brandy, and good conversation." In the same tone with which she'd spoken these banalities, she added: "I have the impression that I've missed the end of the story. Tell me, Licenciado, when you arrived at the restaurant, your chickadee had flown the coop, isn't that right?"

The Millareses waited with near-bated breath for the answer. However, as soon as Dante de la Estrella opened his mouth no one allowed him to answer. All their voices erupted at once. If anyone had been able to decipher the confusion, they'd have heard:

Elenita, Millares's daughter, asking how many Turks could fit inside the Blue Mosque, and whether it was full all the time or only when mass was being celebrated.

Her brother, Juan Ramón, inquiring if the Turkish woman had

belly danced for them at the restaurant, then adding, with delight, how much he'd have liked to see her scar in the shape of a little mouth, and was it true that it opened and closed as if it were singing.

Old man Millares commenting that if the woman had left, they'd certainly have had no difficulty in meeting her any other day. After all, they'd made the trip to Turkey for the express purpose of meeting her. Wasn't that right?

Amelia asking him to explain who'd fallen in love with whom, since from the start she'd sensed that it was a story of difficult relationships, but without being able to clearly place the protagonists.

And Salvador Millares, the architect, stating that he'd missed the most important part of the story. Why had the Licenciado stopped speaking to Rodrigo Vives? Or had it been, as in his case, Rodrigo himself who'd decided to cut off all dealings with him? What had been the problem? Was it also a question of money?

At that moment the maid came in with the coffee and refreshments. Everyone fell silent, as if embarrassed. The Licenciado apologized for not drinking coffee and made himself another whiskey, not as strong as the one before. In the new general silence that followed, he began to eat quickly, in large bites, an enormous slice of tortilla española and to drink his whiskey noisily.

"And then, Licenciado?" Amelia renewed the attack.

"Then *what*?" he answered with a surly tone.

"You didn't answer my question."

"That's right, I didn't answer, and if you rush me, I'll take the liberty of telling you that I don't have to. Among other things, I found your words inexplicable."

"I only asked if your chickadee had flown the coop," she responded, a bit cross.

"And I in turn answer with another question: Exactly what

chickadee was supposed to have flown the coop? It seems as if you believe that I've done nothing but talk about birds, isn't that so? Ducks, hens?" He then added dryly: "By one of those contradictions in which the collective soul is typically so rich, it just so happens that you want to know something about me, you're pressing me to clarify it, and when you've finally vanquished my scruples, you make such a ruckus that I can no longer speak. I've opened up to you. I've told you that this is the first time, and I am sure it will be the last, that I've spoken of the trip. It's not just because I saw that prodigious mosque," he said, pointing to Juan Ramón's jigsaw puzzle, "but, above all, because of the old friendship that unites us; it's possible that something I dreamt last night may also have something to do with it. A nightmare I can't remember, but which must have something to do with this need to connect that is quite unlike me. This entire morning I've experienced a kind of somnambulism, along with a sensation that inside me that sleep that eludes me is still alive and working away at me. Suddenly I felt I had to talk to your wife, Millares, and I happened on that mosque. A clear case of parapsychology! You'll never understand, perhaps because of your obstinacy to not do so, how that trip affected me, not only at the time, which would be normal, but in the years that followed. My life was never the same again. That said, I don't regret going to Istanbul. I complain; I talk about my traumas, my pain, etcetera, but deep down I must admit that in the battle that took place there, I was the only victor. Yes, I was the only winner in that terrible contest. An infinite space opened up to me to develop my spirit. I fear, Millares, that you, reduced as you are by your own inclination for pulp literature, won't be able to understand the pleasure that another kind of book can produce. There is nothing, in my opinion, in the world that surpasses the thirst for knowledge.

Looking for certain works in catalogs that are difficult to obtain, ordering them, waiting impatiently for their arrival. Spending several hours a day engrossed in their company, making notes. I am a different man, despite the efforts of my wife and the world to keep me at ground level. A heroic effort that many don't understand, but whose realization is enough for me."

"So," Amelia insisted, in a much less confident voice, "had the woman left when you arrived at the restaurant?"

"Did they make you try any aphrodisiacs? Those from the East have the reputation of being the best in the world," interrupted Juan Ramón.

"Please leave the Licenciado alone. He's going to tell us if the trip that night was in vain."

De la Estrella looked around him, pausing his blurred gaze on each one of those present. Then, in a shrill voice, he exclaimed:

"You know my obsession with punctuality. It's a mania, I know. There are those who throw it in my face, what can you do. Even on the days and hours when the traffic is heaviest, I'm always on time. It's not a virtue I've endeavored to cultivate; on the contrary, it's a congenital habit, an integral part of my deep nature. I don't need to look at a watch or wait for someone to tell me what time it is to know that I should go the bathroom, that I need to shave faster or slower, what time to put on my tie, when to shut the door of the house and get into the car. I have a precise clockwork mechanism inside me. I leave the house at the right time and arrive at my destination at the right time. That's how I am, that's how I've been for as long as I can remember, and that's how I'll be until the day I die. If I'm invited to dinner at eight o'clock in the evening, rest assured that I'll arrive at my hosts' home at exactly the time specified, which leads me to always find the people at home in their shirtsleeves, then having to

wait a couple of hours for the other guests to arrive. This fastidious-
ness is irritating for those who comment, to justify their internal
disorder, that it's an obsolete habit on my part, ridiculous, affected.
At the end of the day, they end up not inviting me anymore. They
don't know the favor they're doing me, that my studies and I come
out on top. But why does Dante de la Estrella, Esquire, who com-
pleted a postgraduate year in Rome, boast about certain qualities
of his if he was telling us about a trip to Turkey? Has he lost his
way? Has he been infected by his wife's contradictions and those of
other people with whom, against his will, he's forced to associate?
There are those who wish it were that way. I take great delight in
disappointing them. If I speak of my preoccupation with punctuality, it is so that you understand the humiliation I experienced that
night, the distress of arriving when Marietta Karapetiz had been
waiting for us for an hour and a half."

"So you found her at last? Who would have thought it!"

"You should know, señora, that any hotel that boasts of having five stars always has at its disposal a more or less efficient cab
service. All except the one where we stayed. The Pera Palace was
then still a place of considerable prestige. It was mentioned in novels and diaries of important authors; its image appeared in several
American movies, and yet, I was unaware of the existence of those
indispensable services that any Mexican hotel with fewer stars
makes available to its clientele. A doorman told me that the cab
had been ordered and that it would pick us up at any moment. 'A
black Buick,' he said, 'winking at me, who knows why. But there
was no black Buick, no blue Buick, no purple Buick; no Ford, no
Volkswagen, no mule, no camel. Finally, I asked a bellhop to go out
to the street to get a car. He returned with it at the time we were
supposed to be at the restaurant. Who could remember now if it

was a Buick, let alone black! All I can tell you is that it was very old and very dirty, and its interior smelled to high heaven. Ramona handed the driver a card with the name and address of the place where we were going. Placing trust in a Turk, I can assure you, is the biggest mistake anyone could ever make in life. The boy who'd gone to get the car was expecting I don't know what kind of fabulous tip, and when I handed him the few Italian coins left in my pocket, he threw them on the floor, mumbling an indecency in his incomprehensible language. His very tone and the knowing looks he exchanged with the driver made me extremely uneasy. I have no doubt that as soon as the car drove off, he bent down to pick up the coins. I've never believed the fervent words and gestures of those who claim to despise money. For half an hour we drove through the city in various directions. At last we left it. We drove past the great bridge over the Bosporus and came to a beach lined with restaurants and nightclubs. Our car stopped. I thought we'd arrived. I was about to open the door and jump out into the street when I realized that we were trapped in yet another of the many embarrassing situations that made up that accursed journey. The driver turned to us and began to speak to us in Turkish. Who could understand him? English and Italian, not to mention our sovereign language, were of no use to us. From the gestures he made toward nearby restaurants, from the city guide where he inquisitively showed us the dining section, we understood that he was asking for the name and address of the restaurant we were looking for. We told them that we'd given him this information on a card. No matter, he didn't understand; that is, he pretended not to understand us. Ramona tore a blank sheet of paper out of her appointment book, took out her fountain pen, and pretended to write a few words; then she passed the paper to him. She was trying to reproduce the gesture he made when she handed the driver the first address card. The Turk took the paper, looked at both sides with a puzzled face, making us understand that he saw nothing, and then, with a grimace of indescribable vulgarity, he put his hands to his temples, and made an unmistakable gesture that suggested that Ramona wasn't in her right mind and that, as a man, he was holding me responsible for the situation. His tone was becoming quite aggressive. It was like a scene from a madhouse! He began to drive the car; we sped along for a few blocks, reading each of the neon signs. At one point the cab pulled into a dark alley. I was sure, and my instinct has never failed me, that this nasty character had made an agreement with the hotel bellhop to rob us; I had no doubt he could have called other hooligans, who were waiting for us in that narrow and abandoned alley to clean us out. It would be easy to make the robbery look accidental. I became very nervous, but I didn't allow myself to lose my head. I quickly pulled out a fifty-dollar bill and showed it to the driver. The mobster took out a flashlight and studied it carefully. At that moment, as if by magic, the light stopped on a spot in the car where a crumpled piece of paper lay next to the hand brake; he held it up, looking surprised, and, of course, it was ours, with the name and address of the restaurant we were looking for. He tried to take the money, but, with the speed of an illusionist, I managed to snatch it from his hands and told him that when we arrived at the restaurant, we would give him an excellent tip. He seemed to understand that his game had been discovered and that he had no choice but to act accordingly. I don't want to dwell on this incident. Suffice it to say that it was almost ten o'clock when we met Marietta Karapetiz. And our appointment was for half past eight!"

"Well, well, well! That Turkish woman must really have loved Rodrigo Vives to wait for him until that hour! Was she disappointed to discover that her soulmate sent his ambassadors to meet her?" asked the architect in a sort of mocking tone.

"I've never said that Marietta Karapetiz was Turkish, rather that she lived in Turkey, in Istanbul, to be more precise. I would appreciate if you would refrain from distorting my words with your imagination. I'm trying to be precise in each and every incident involved in that absurd but revealing episode of my life. I ask, then, and I believe I have the right to do so, that you refrain from expressing your own interpretations," replied De la Estrella bitingly. "In effect, we were in front of the restaurant where the person you call 'the Turkish woman' was waiting for us, although I can't say patiently. I jumped out of the cab. With the utmost courtesy I informed Ramona that while she settled with the driver, I'd go ahead in order to find our guest and offer the customary explanations. I didn't even wait for her reply, rather rushed into the restaurant. I explained in Italian to the maître d', who fortunately understood me immediately, that we'd reserved a table in the name of Señor Vives, who was staying at the Pera Palace, for four people, and that a lady might have been waiting for us for quite some time. 'Of course, of course, for a very long time!' he answered rather haughtily, in my opinion, and ordered a waiter to take me to our table. As amazing as it may seem, but I must say that insofar as she's concerned one was always faced with the extraordinary, still seated there was the now oft-mentioned Marietta Karapetiz. It's difficult for me to describe my first impression. She almost frightened me. Her face was that of a toucan; but that image vanished instantly, because apart from the nose, she had none of the traits one might attribute to those cheerful tropical birds. She was instead like a giant crow with a prominent nose, yes, like a toucan, but at the same time she had the appearance of a massive safe. No, please,

I ask you again not to rush to offer your own versions, it couldn't be said that the widow Karapetiz was fat, but rather compact, hermetic, rather square-shouldered; a concentration of flesh, I would say, imprisoned in a shimmering black moiré dress. I have no qualms in stating again: She frightened me. She was surrounded by an orchestra of Gypsies. The first violinist's bow was almost caressing her furiously black hair. She was humming, with an absent and somber air, a song. I approached the table with a not very determined step. She looked at me with a disinterest that suggested she didn't see me. I reached her and held out my hand. She stopped me in my tracks with a stern, military gesture; she raised her voice and continued singing. At the end of the piece, she dismissed the musicians with an enormous if somewhat melancholy smile and a few words in Turkish. There was no familiarity between them. Quite the opposite; she carried herself like a grande dame, a matriarchal figure, obliging, generous, but still imperious. She turned to me and with extreme sternness informed me that the table was occupied, that she wouldn't accept company. 'Go away! Get out!' she shouted at me in English. It's possible that she thought I wished to take liberties with her. If so, that would explain much of what happened next. Is it possible that I'd frightened her, despite the fact that she'd spent her whole life traveling the world? I'm not quite sure. The truth is, I've rarely encountered such a hostile reception. Fortunately, just then Ramona arrived. She walked from the door to our table, stumbling and with a frightened look on her face, her mouth moving wildly, as if she were talking to herself but not making any sounds. I imagined the hard time she must've had with the driver. Who knows what kind of fortune he got for driving us for an hour and a half against our will through the worst neighborhoods of Istanbul! But I was determined to not feel guilty, to not allow myself to be blackmailed by her histrionics. Had they invited me to see Turkey, or was there another motive? The Viveses, I'd soon realized, were a pair of capricious, boastful, and exceedingly ungrateful siblings. I'll see to it that they don't forget, I told myself. Finally, without allowing me to speak, Ramona began to explain incoherently to the autocrat who we were. With a martial gesture, just like the one she'd used to stop me from approaching her, she pointed to two seats, and continued to hum, without musicians, the same song she'd sung. Her first words, when she finally decided it was time to speak, couldn't have been more unfriendly: 'Well, well, Mexicans! I know your country. I imagine you are aware of this . . . *¡México lindo y querido, si muero lejos de ti . . . !* I know my people! Tomorrow, tomorrow, always tomorrow! Don't do today what you can put off for the next millennium! To think that I almost became a Mexican! I had only a moment of doubt. They wanted to turn me into a charrita from the very Highlands of Jalisco, but it wasn't possible, I was already married, I have always been faithful. I am by nature. I have no regrets, nothing of the sort. Rather than an arrogant charra attached for a short time to the massive harem of a lecherous louse, I decided to be a sweet and humble chilanguita, the lady of the house next door on the centrally located Calle de la Palma, number ninety-five, apartment seven. I give thanks to the holy and most miraculous Virgencita de los Remedios, and the Santo Niño de Chalma, and, of course, and above all things, our mother Tonāntzin, the virgin par excellence, the morenita, the guadalupana Empress of America, for having saved me from being reduced to tomorrow and next year, patroncitos, and for having maintained come hell or high water my belief in the modest present, our daily today! *¡Olé torero!*' I could only wonder if we were dealing with a madwoman, or if by that time the Professor was drowning in her cups. Ramona Vives, truly embarrassed by the rather bizarre reception, began with a shrill, monotonous, and submissive voice, typical of girls of the Sagrado Corazón, to explain from the beginning what had happened—Rodrigo's malaise from the moment he arrived at the station, his sudden illness a few hours later, his boundless desire to greet her, see her, hear her; she failed to say: smell her. He wanted to consult with her, she added, on certain papers he considered fundamental to his studies. 'You are the real purpose of our journey, dear Professor, our beginning and our end. You can't imagine my brother's devotion, what am I saying, his fervor for your husband's work and for your brilliance, which is unparalleled! Yes, Marietta,' she started, presumptuously, to call her by her first name—if that was her first name! 'Rodrigo has told us so much about you, your essays, your lectures.'"

"A rather amusing situation, it seems," Salvador Millares commented.

"Is that what you think?" De la Estrella asked in his most pedantic voice. "Perhaps from a distance, from the outside, it might seem amusing, but I assure you that experiencing it in the flesh was not. While Ramona was repeating and magnifying in the most convoluted way all of Rodrigo's praise for Marietta and Aram Karapetiz, and adding some of her own, Karapetiz was paying close attention, weighing each word, measuring its scope, while at the same time scrutinizing with the rapacious eye of a pawnbroker the young Ramona's attire and jewelry; she began to caress a silver brooch with blue inlays, perhaps lapis lazuli, and asked if that beautiful piece was Mexican. I don't remember exactly Ramona's response. I think she explained that the brooch was Egyptian, that she had bought it from an antique dealer in New York. I'm not sure. What I do know is that as soon as Marietta Karapetiz withdrew her hand,

Ramona removed it from her chest and placed it on one of the upper corners of the dress that made its owner look like an impregnable safe. The celebrated humanist accepted the gift with unthinkable shamelessness. She didn't put up the slightest resistance, not even for the sake of feigning the most elementary decorum. She accepted it as a tribute, which didn't even seem to satisfy her very much. She took a mirror out of her handbag and coolly studied the position of the brooch. She repositioned it several times to complement her necklaces of thick silver beads. She finally decided on the right place. Even in her way of giving thanks, her odd vulgarity of taste stood out: 'A thousand thanks I give you, *Santísima Señora del Oponoxtle*, for not forsaking me on this day that was so fateful.'"

"And you say that woman wasn't amusing!" Millares's father interrupted. De la Estrella looked at him loathingly, but the old man didn't flinch. "In my opinion, a woman who waits in a restaurant for more than an hour and a half and is still in the mood to joke is worth more than a silver mine."

"Appearances! Façade! If you'd known her better, you'd keep those remarks to yourself, which, allow me to say, I like less and less, as I find them rather suspiciously similar to certain zarzuela dialogues with mocking intentions. Your sneers, I wish to make it clear, toward a man such as I, who has long since reached, perhaps by force of circumstance, but reached after all, a certain age, do not affect me."

"Come on, take it easy! I ... !"

"Yes, señor, let's leave it there. I believed that the initial bad moment had passed, that the ice had been broken, so I took the opportunity to introduce myself properly and to give her my business card. She read it quietly, then repeated it aloud, scanning each syllable: 'Dante C. de la Estrella, Doctor in Law, Via Vittoria thirty-six, Rome.' I hadn't yet obtained the title of doctor, well, I never obtained it, why not say it, is that perhaps a crime? But it didn't seem serious to me that the card introduced me as such, since at that time I was certain that it would be a matter of a few more months before I finished my doctorate. It wasn't. I had return to Mexico in a rush, for reasons that aren't relevant, but which I also have no reason to hide. I got married. It's no secret to anyone. It was a forced marriage. Karapetiz's widow, with the card still in hand, examined me with barely concealed disdain. She smiled something akin to a snake's smile and finally asked: 'Is it a pseudonym?' only to add with the same mocking tone before I could answer: 'What secret is hidden behind the letter C?' I was thunderstruck, speechless in the face of the gratuitousness of that unexpected attack. I'd suggested to everyone that that C was short for César, the name of my maternal grandfather. I never liked my middle name. I never use it. The C appeared by mistake all because a friend at the Mexican Consulate, who gave the name to the printer just as it appeared in my passport, wanted to give me those cards as a gift on my birthday. I hoped to ignore the insidious question, so I began to stress my firm belief in punctuality, tell her about the shocks we experienced in the cab, but she drew me back to her interrogation with the ruthless air of a prosecutor: 'So is it a pseudonym, Don Dante?' I shook my head, bemused; I tried to return to the story about the cab, but there it was, steely, implacable, the dreaded question: 'And the C? That precious and dear little letter C, what does it stand for? Does it perhaps evoke the name of our Savior? Anything is possible nowadays, although it seems a bit excessive, don't you think?' I was going to reply with a sharp retort. In those days, I was young and spirited, and some of my responses were more effective than a hook to the liver, but Ramona Vives beat me to the punch with her hateful voice of a Piarist sister at convent school: 'No, Marietta, as strange as it may seem, it's not a pseudonym. Dante is his real name. And the C that so rightly intrigues you stands for Ciriaco.' I was petrified. How could she know that? From her brother, of course, but even so, how, where, when had Rodrigo Vives found out that my middle name was Ciriaco? The blow that she inflicted was so devastating that for an instant it paralyzed the energy of each and every one of my cells. Anyone who speaks of having experienced clinical death must know a sensation similar to the one I experienced at that moment. It was a miracle I didn't fall to the floor. I'd spent my whole life hiding that name, and it had become such common knowledge that a woman I'd met just the day before was shouting it in a nightspot in Istanbul. I thought of the rude jokes my classmates had made at my expense, and the recent ones with which Rodrigo surely mocked me to Ramona in their luxury compartment: 'Look, fratellita, the guy who joined us in Venice, his name isn't just Dante; he completely obliterates that glorious name with one that is even more laughable. Do you know what his middle name is? Ciriaco! Dante Ciriaco! What do you think of that?' And they probably burst out laughing. My face was burning, my temples were throbbing, my heart was pounding. I showed a strength of character that surprised even me. Not only did I not fall to the floor in convulsions, but I decided to cross the bridge, with my head held high, and finish the explanation I'd begun regarding our difficulties with the cab driver. 'Had we known that Rodrigo had chosen a restaurant so far from the city,' I observed, 'we would have picked you up so we could all arrive together. That way, in the event that you had to wait for us, you would have done so in your home with all the necessary comforts.' I don't know if she interpreted my remarks as a slight barb at the Viveses for their inattentiveness or not. What's certain is that she not only mocked me in her response but was manifestly rude, saying that she had chosen the place, and not Rodrigo, who is always attentive, always a gentleman, so studious, so wise, so similar in his habits to Doctor Karapetiz, 'which is the highest praise I allow myself to pay to a living person,' and the reason she chose that place was precisely because it was just a step away from her home. She began to protest at the top of her lungs, even though her protestations mattered to no one, that she couldn't tolerate cities, neither large nor small, or even medium-sized ones. She was pure Nature. She needed the sea, the sky, and the mountains. And the rivers and the jungle. And there she had the sea just a stone's throw away. She could see it, smell it, feel its effects on her skin, drink it through her pores. 'When my husband became ill, I managed to convince him that we should settle here. His illness was untreatable, and I knew it. Was there any point in living in Ankara, where the only thing that interested us was the University, which he could no longer visit? Here we would have not only doctors, but also the sea. I live a stone's throw from this little place where I often come to eat and drink. If I'd known you would arrive so late, I'd have soaked in the bathtub for an hour in camel's milk, the best remedy for softening the complexion and hardening the viscera.' She loved to spout such bunk, worthy of an itinerant clown, which she pretended to pass off as Gongoresque wit. Fortunately, something caught her eye in Ramona's dress. She began to feel the fabric of the sleeves, to ask I don't know what about the needlework. She made my companion stand up, take a few steps to one side, to the other, in order to see how the skirt hung in the back. Only at that moment, when I believed I was out of Marietta Karapetiz's spotlight, was I able to look around, and I noticed that the place was much more elegant than I'd assumed. Most of the women were in evening attire, and I, dressed in shirtsleeves and khaki pants, was the only guest who brought a note of informality to the group, which tends to make one look out of place. If there's anyone who feels conspicuous, it's a tramp in a house full of swells. I felt like a rube, which further heightened my annoyance in the company of that pair of dolled-up floozies. I excused myself for a moment, but they didn't even notice! I went to the bathroom; I stopped at the bar to buy cigarettes and glanced at the crowd. I needed to escape from the stale air of our table, to breathe new life into my lungs. When I came back, Ramona was going on, for a change, about the difficult time she was going through, the existential anguish she was experiencing, having not yet chosen a topic for her thesis. She recounted how the previous night, while dining on the Orient Express, the notion of anthropology as a great contribution to literary knowledge had risen on her cultural horizon. Marietta Karapetiz listened to her not only patiently but also attentively, though apparently not excessively, because at my compatriot's first pause, she nodded her head and instead of contributing to the subject, as would have been the logical thing to do, she asked mercurially what we'd seen that morning in Istanbul. 'Very little,' we said in unison, and started talking at the same time. The woman lost her patience. She raised one arm—the right one, I believe—stretched out the palm of her hand, and imposed silence on us. She delivered, without our having asked, an extensive description of the city, its historical legacy. She spoke of the extant fragments of its walls, of the Christian churches and mosques, of the intersection of different cultures, languages, religions, of the extreme ethnic complexity. I didn't expect it, so I was surprised by the quality and pleasantness of her presentation. Before I realized it, I was enraptured listening to her.

Was there really any greatness in her words? Perhaps it only seemed so at the time. I was very young, very naïve in many respects, and could mistake truculence for oratorical excellence. I allowed myself to comment during a pause that when I saw the people in the restaurant I felt as if I were in a nice place in Mexico. 'Yes, señor,' she answered me tersely, 'your observation is very correct. The two countries have more than one thing in common.' Do you see? For the first time she acknowledged that something I'd said might be close to right. 'Almost every type of person that can be found here could be found in my multifaceted and precious Mexico. But there are also more subtle similarities between both worlds, more recondite, that only an extremely sensitive mind, and I didn't imagine that yours was one, would know how to grasp.' And then she added something that left me bewildered: 'Several centuries ago, Constantine Porphyrogenitus revealed that only when shit, which in the end is fire, breaks its pact with the devil can it become nourishing, fecundating breath.' I thought I'd misunderstood a word, I need not explain which, and I dared to ask her: 'Could you tell me, Professor, what fire was for the person you mentioned?' And she, with the greatest composure in the world, while raising her wine glass in front of me, bringing it to her lips and licking it rather than drinking from it, answered me, with relish, 'Shit.' 'Shit,' she repeated again, punctuating the *t*, 'by freeing itself from its diabolical pact would, according to him, end up becoming a nourishing element, a fecundating breath.' You can imagine my bewilderment! How was I supposed to take that? I thought that my stay in Rome had transformed me into a man of the world incapable of being surprised by anything. At that moment I felt as if several light-centuries separated me from such a goal. To conceal my bafflement, I also raised my glass and swallowed its contents in a single gulp. I looked at

Ramona as if searching for help. Was I suffering from an auditory hallucination? Hearing voices? What, on the other hand, had the priggish Señorita Vives heard? Apparently not the same as I, since she was inserting, with total serenity, I could almost say sensually, a long, fat asparagus into her mouth with her slender little fingers, without sharing any of my uneasiness. To get out of the fix, I had no choice but to turn the rudder. I commented with feigned nonchalance that she'd not yet told us anything about the moments, I was going to say sublime, but I stopped myself in time because the adjective seemed inappropriate, that she'd experienced in Mexico. I asked her to consider us to be as worthy of listening to her as was Rodrigo Vives, who, he'd told us, had enjoyed her memoirs immensely. We knew from him that one of her trips had coincided with some revolutionary event that impeded her husband's research, and on a mere whim of the moment, without thinking, just to brighten the conversation, because deep down I didn't care a fig, I asked her if they'd traveled to Mexico from Istanbul. Had they embarked from here? 'And why Istanbul?' she blurted out like a wild cat. 'Where did you get such an outlandish idea? We didn't live here; I could never have imagined at the time that I would one day become stranded on this reef.' 'Please don't be upset,' I shot back, 'I imagine that if one is Turkish, it would be logical to embark from a Turkish port, don't you think so, my dear?'"

Dante de la Estrella turned his eyes to his audience and asked if any of those present considered his question an anomaly.

"No, not really," answered Amelia Millares, rather lost.

"If one meets a person in Turkey, hears them speak the language of the country, and they have the same appearance as the locals, the most logical thing would be to think that the person is Turkish, don't you think?"

There was a silence, interrupted only by a sort of throat-clearing from Don Antonio Millares, with which he seemed to agree vaguely with the guest's contention. De la Estrella seemed dissatisfied with the response. He looked inquisitively at the others in search of something more resounding. When he didn't receive it, he insisted in a pettish voice:

"Was I right or was I wrong?"

"They say that everyone," exclaimed Salvador Millares with glee, "sooner or later meets their match. And it looks like you found yours with that apocalyptic Turkish woman."

"Who said that?"

"Goethe, I believe."

"If I may, neither you nor Goethe know what you're talking about. It wasn't a wasted experience. I discovered many things, among them my vocation as a polemicist. What a monumental lesson that was! If someone asks me from what deep source sprang the series of essays I published years later in the magazine *Todo*, I would answer that it wasn't from the University, nor from my stay in Rome, but rather that I discovered it during the two days I spent in the Turkish capital. I should remind you all that it's still the night of that never-ending first day. You'll have noticed by now from my account that Marietta Karapetiz possesses a refined expertise in rebuffs, but on that occasion, she went too far, and how! 'Turk!' she shouted, pursing her face, closing her eyes like an irate monkey, frightened and contemptuous. When she opened them, she looked at me as if I were a rat, a cockroach, a repellent insect. Her look made me so nervous that my hands began to tremble, and I could barely manage to pour myself more wine. 'People come up to me,' she began to say at last, 'they tell me their names if they choose, since it's not an obligation I impose on anyone. It doesn't matter

too much whether those names have a certain dignity or whether
they are, and it is not my wish to offend those present, simply grotesque; they tell me where they come from, they talk because they
choose to, I never question them. I'm not interested in knowing
whether they were born only the devil knows where, on what street
or in what fetid roadside ditch. It's none of my business, nor anyone else's, except the person concerned. Did I ask you, by chance,
your nationality? You told me you were Mexican. Very well, I
believe you. I take you at your word. I'm not subjecting you to an
interrogation. That's not my personality. No one to date has called
me María Inquisición! I received a correct and proper upbringing,
and I've maintained it with little effort. Turkish, Spanish, Greek
from Alexandria, Circassian, Paraguayan! You choose the nationality that your fantasy dictates to you, since it intrigues you so much.
Do you want me to be Assyrian? No, señor, I won't allow it! Don't
put me in the wrong place. And be very careful; I have those who
defend me,' she spoke with an excitement, with a fury that could
have frightened the devil. 'I'm not a Phoenician either. Get that
into your head. I haven't given anyone a reason to label me as such.
Others may be, not me.' Her words were propelled by such a breath
that I thought I was staring at a cobra, no, an enraged python. By
then it wasn't nerves that were making my hands tremble. The fear
had disappeared. If I was trembling at all, it was out of anger. How
could that crazed tart dare to insult me in such a way?! I was on the
verge of causing a scandal, of throwing the contents of my glass in
her face, insulting her obscenely just as she deserved, and leaving
the establishment. A saving thought restrained me. Such behavior
would have been tantamount to lowering myself to her level. She
was unworthy of such a reaction. At that moment her character was
revealed to me with dazzling clarity: I was sitting before not only a

poor halfwit, but above all, and this is what ultimately disqualified her in my eyes, an unworthy woman. If a lady, I thought, has a modicum of respect for herself, she doesn't wait an hour and a half alone in a restaurant, entertaining herself by singing at the top of her lungs with local musicians, no matter how much she swears that having been a humble neighbor in apartment seven at Calle de la Palma, number ninety-five, had accustomed her to Mexican unpunctuality. A real lady would have returned home furious and offended to await a large bouquet of flowers the next day and apologies from those who'd stood her up. She would then decide whether to accept or reject them. That was her problem. That was what it meant to be a lady and not a madwoman born 'only the devil knows in what fetid roadside ditch.' She very likely arrived at the table, started drinking alcohol with a certain abandon, stuffed herself on hors d'oeuvres, and then succumbed to the panic of having to pay for what she'd consumed. Better to wait until closing time hoping for a miracle than to open her wallet and pay as God intended! I know the sort that belongs to that filthy crowd! I watched her gobble down her turkey with fiendish eyes. The table was filled with large plates, medium-sized plates, small plates, overflowing with delicacies: eggplant and chickpea purées, cheeses of different kinds, sturgeon, caviar of two colors, legumes in mustard and sour cream sauces, bunches of fragrant herbs, pistachios, pine nuts, almonds. She ate her turkey, but at the same time took bites of everything else. She stretched across the table, smelled every dish, even ours, stretched out her arms as if wanting to take it all in. In those moments she'd ceased to be a toucan or a crow and had become an opossum, a voracious anteater whose huge nose threatened to plunge into the sauce boats. She smelled and ate and never stopped talking. You must have noticed by now that she was an incorrigible chatterbox. All of a sudden she abandoned the absurd screed with which she had tried to intimidate me and made some comment about the watermelon-colored shoes that Ramona was wearing. In the blink of an eye, both women pulled their feet out from under the table and began to show them to each other. Ramona Vives's shoes seemed to have been made of some ignoble material, a kind of cardboard covered with plastic, whose garish color cheapened them even more; Marietta Karapetiz's were made of dark snake-skin, with an iridescent effect, and, like everything she was wear-ing, were of good design. 'Unto Caesar what is Caesar's!' I said to myself, without thinking that she could very easily have borrowed them from a shoe store. I know ladies who take dresses out of the stores, for all to see, or borrow them from a rich neighbor to go to a wedding, to the theater, to dine out. Both seemed to soften under the effects of their frivolity; they talked about the toes, the heels, the curve of the instep. One said she had a pair of boots with ceramic buttons that were darling, the other mentioned a breath-taking pair of slippers with transparent heels that looked like real rock crystal, with opaline-winged butterflies on the toes; both paid boundless compliments to Italian fashion, and French couture, and Spanish shoes, with their first-rate suedes and felts, and they cooed and sighed and moved their feet and eyes like pinwheels as they continued to devour the victuals with unimaginable voracity. I was and wasn't there. I heard them without seeing them completely. I began to regain my calm during the ceasefire, to relax. I picked up the silverware and began to eat the turkey I'd barely tasted and to continue savoring a strong and aromatic wine ordered by Marietta Karapetiz, which was a delight. To tell the truth, I don't know if for an instant I half dozed off or just escaped the conversation to save my soul. What's certain is that when I heard that unmuzzled magpie again, she was talking about some lectures she'd been giving every winter for the last four or five years at American universities. Another transformation! I found myself sitting in front of Doctor Jekyll-Karapetiz; solemn, severe, even her gaze seemed to have been transformed. When I emerged from my lethargy, I had the sensation of listening to an evangelist missionary preaching. In recent times, she declared, she'd decided to speak almost exclusively about Gogol. She claimed to know almost everything of any importance that had been written or said about that writer, and to have discovered on her own one or two new things. When I recall the seriousness with which she made such statements, I don't know whether to laugh or cry. She commented that a few days before she'd just corrected the proofs of a book that was about to appear with the Presses universitaires de France. Soon it would also be published by an American university press. She claimed to work like a lioness and decided to ignore me. She had ears only for herself. At the end of the summer, she was to read a paper, something very simple, she said, a modest chronicle of the death of Nikolai Vasilyevich, at an international meeting of Slavicists to be held in Verona. A subject that lent itself to deploying all the imagination and fantasy one could muster, given that the stage seemed to be drawn from his own work, especially his early stories, in which Satan and his abominable progeny played a central role, stories that some scholars, especially the acerbic Nabokov, viewed with contempt as mere learning exercises, games to loosen the hand, while she considered that there was already in those Ukrainian stories the germ of the prodigious author who would write *Dead Souls* years later, and that they were in themselves small masterpieces, indispensable to understand the spirit that animated the writer's entire work. Yes, as soon as I began to listen to that speech, I understood that there coexisted in that woman several personalities, that of Doctor Jekyll, Mister Hyde, Marietta Karapetiz, and who knows how many others. Each of the creatures that inhabited her spoke a different language, behaved in a different way, their gestures and manners were different. During those moments, everything about her was strict, measured, professional. She pointed out that whoever wanted to delve into his rich work should spend time on a text often undervalued by scholars, discussed ad nauseum, always on the basis of erroneous insights. 'The Old World Landowners' was the title. Already during the author's lifetime, critics were radically divided in their judgment of this story. The eternal nonconformists, that eternally accursed race, good only for disrupting order, hurled at Gogol all the mud in which their souls wallowed. What irritated them, drove them mad with fury, about a text that any uninformed reader would consider an innocent vignette of rural life? What made them foam at the mouth? One simple reason. They accused the author of being a staunch defender of feudal customs, including the regime of serfdom, for the simple act of describing the daily life of an elderly married couple, their games at home, their peaceful customs, the innocent jokes with which they entertained themselves to pass the time. As for the self-righteous, who sometimes, I must admit, are often blinded, they accused Gogol of the opposite, of denigrating the owners of the estates through this senile couple. A constant jeering, they argued, a relentless mockery of values established by tradition. They thought it insulting for the rural lords to see themselves personified in that pair of old simpletons. For them, the story boiled down to that. The gaps between the Professor Jekyll-Hyde-Karapetiz were in some respects inconceivable, oceanic. In almost none of her essays does she refer to this polemic, which in itself explains an entire epoch of Russian culture.

When she spoke of 'the landowners,' she became lost in a veritable word salad that at times was nearly impenetrable: Eros! Thanatos! The libido as salvation! The libido as condemnation! Fashionable fluff! Pedantry! Pure farce!"

"And couldn't that also have its interest?"

There was no response. Like a sleepwalker, Dante C. de la Estrella made his way to the drink table. He made himself another whiskey and soda, tasted it, smacked his lips, and moved his head from side to side, unhappy with the results. He put another ice cube in the glass, took another long drink, apparently more satisfying than the last. Returning to his seat, he made a visual inspection of the audience. He was on the verge of spilling his whiskey. With the exception of the architect, who was no longer reading, but whose head was thrown back, his eyes closed and an expressionless smile on his mouth, gently rocking in his chair, the others had returned to their petty distractions: cards, crocheting, the Taj Mahal, the Blue Mosque. So he'd spent his time casting pearls before swine? The denizens of that pigsty only became excited when someone descended to their level, immune to any emotion that held the slightest spark of wit. He'd tried to elevate them to another world, and he was witnessing his failure. Their attention was aroused only by their proximity to the lower fray, pedestrian love affairs, scarred bellies and not entirely closed wounds. His mind grew dim. He walked mechanically to his seat and fell backward, as he'd done before, in the exact middle of the sofa. His head tilted even more; his glassy eyes swept, as if shooting daggers, over the flock that had no possibility of redemption. At last, he seemed to exit his paralysis. Had his disquisitions on the Russian author bored them? "Be careful what you ask for," he seemed to say to himself. In a metallic, disagreeable voice, he asked:

"Have you ever read Gogol, Millares?"

The architect appeared to wake up from his blissful daydream. He settled for a mocking smile and showed the Licenciado the novel by Simenon he was holding in his hands. Then, without adding a word, he opened it and did his best to read it.

Don Antonio Millares commented that he'd read him, yes, but a thousand years ago.

"*Dead Souls*, of course; that was what I read. Now, if you ask me what it's about, it would be hard for me to say. I remember that the main character was a rather bizarre man who traveled the roads of old Russia in search of dead people to buy. Isn't that it? For what purpose, I don't have slightest idea. For my generation, reading the Russians was almost compulsory. I left off with Andreyev, it seems to me."

"And I, on the other hand," Dante de la Estrella interrupted him abruptly with a triumphant and spiteful voice, "I've read all of him, from beginning to end, not once but several times. Whoever says that I did it to emulate Marietta Karapetiz is lying! God forbid! I was never her follower or disciple. On the contrary. I was her most careful reader, that's true, but also the most demanding. I became, to say it quickly, her most implacable critic, her true scourge. I acutely demonstrated, supported by a weighty apparatus of erudition, that she and everything that emanated from her was nothing but an unremitting fraud. When the time came, I read her book on Gogol. I didn't miss the subsequent essays she published in American and Canadian academic journals. Not a single one!" He let out a short, dry, hateful laugh. "Without mercy, because in the fields of knowledge one must be implacable. I demonstrated with irrefutable arguments a thousand errors underlying a prose that was mere sparks of nothingness, tinsel. Yes, ladies and gentlemen,

I've not only devoured the complete works of the great Nikolai Vasilyevich Gogol, but also a good part of what has been published about him in English, Italian, and Spanish, which is no small feat, I can assure you. As you know, at one time I systematically published my articles. Do you remember the magazine *Todo*? I was initiated in that very esteemed publication. A cabal of intriguing and envious people closed that once generous door to me. However, I didn't surrender. I continued to publish my philippics in the form of Letters to the Editor in various newspapers and magazines in the capital, and especially in the provinces, which is where people read the most. I informed the interested party of everything I published. Some phrases must have incensed her because she never sent me as much as a reply in her defense, not even the briefest acknowledgment of receipt." He took a sip of his whiskey; then, once again disoriented, asked: "Now, why am I saying this?"

"You were telling us that you'd dined in a restaurant outside Istanbul?"

"Oh, yes? Do you think I left off there? I don't know why, but I have the impression of having gone much further," said De la Estrella, resentful.

"Hombre!" Don Antonio interjected, always conciliatory. "You were saying that the overly chatty professor was talking to you, while you were eating, about some of Gogol's books that critics tend to dismiss."

"Precisely! Marietta Karapetiz launched into a discourse on Nikolai Vasilyevich Gogol's early stories. Not those full of witches, devils, spells, terrifying goblins, unbridled heroism, and lots of cheap blood, which can't be ignored either, rather his fanciful parodies of everyday life, 'Ivan Fyodorovich Shponka and His Aunt,' for example, or 'The Tale of How Ivan Ivanovich Quarreled with

Ivan Nikiforovich,' but she spoke most about 'The Old World Landowners.' She said that in these stories, without having to resort to the satanic paraphernalia of earlier stories, nor to that rather pre-fabricated carnivalesque magic with which he imbued Ukrainian legends, the hallucinatory somnambulistic element was already emerging, the taste for immoderation that foreshadowed the later Gogol, that of the undisputed masterpieces."

He paused again, looked around, as if frightened, as if his memory had failed him at that moment and he was waiting for a prompter to emerge from somewhere to dictate the continuation of the speech.

"And what did this element consist of?" asked old man Millares, trying to unblock him.

"Wait, please wait, allow me a moment of respite. I greatly appreciate your interest, but in life, my friend, everything has a nat-ural rhythm. Allow me to remind you that if curiosity killed the cat, haste crippled the horse. If you knew into what dark jungle I began to enter, into what abyss I fell, you'd understand, perhaps, the rea-son for my caution! Only my fortitude, a willpower worthy of titans, managed to rescue me. During that talk, Marietta Karapetiz posited a thesis that she later reiterated on many occasions, as I was able to prove when I read her book and some of her articles, and which constituted the starting point of some reflections as complex in their enunciation as they were meager in their con-tent. What element did she detect as primordial, you may rightly ask. In those passages of idyllic life, she stubbornly attempted to discover a perverse substratum, boiling over with contradictions, confusing, rooted in a libido as unbridled as misguided. A sexu-ality at once intensely awake and frightened. Immersed in a sex-ual miasma that she knew to perfection, from personal experience,

I'm certain, and forgetting where we were, Marietta Karapetiz began to deliver her lecture. She got up on an imaginary platform, I think she even stopped eating, and launched into an analysis of the old-world landowners. To tell the truth, on that occasion she left me bewildered; later, when I studied those theses that she'd expanded at greater length in her book, I found them so pretentious and absurd that I decided to refute them in writing. I rebutted her with an energy that, I'm sure, she'd never known, accustomed as she was to the incense of her coryphaei, yes, to the perpetual applause of the servile acolytes. I remember that article with special emotion, because with it I began a work of years, interrupted only recently, as a writer. You don't know that story, I understand, so I'll allow myself to summarize it in a few words. You must imagine an old married couple, already closer to the Great Beyond than to this world: Afanasy Ivanovich and Pulkheria Ivanovna. They live disconnected from the surrounding world, oblivious to everything moving around them. Their only activity consists of eating from sunrise to sunset. At the home of this blessed old couple a meal is served every hour or every two hours, even at night. Their home is their fortress. The couple doesn't enjoy or even notice their possessions. They'd be dumbstruck if someone were to ask them what the oil painting hanging on the left side of the living room window represents, or the other two small ones adorning the walls of the dining room. They've never stopped to gaze at them. The paintings for them are like a series of tiny fly droppings stuck to the walls where they live. All they care about are the eight or nine meals they gobble and digest during the day. 'The simulacrum of life that is represented in this incorporeal and excrementitious environment,' wrote Karapetiz, 'must, by necessity, be barren and insipid.' Besides her husband, Pulkheria Ivanovna loves a gentle cat that is her companion and that, when doing her chores, lies at her feet like a ball. One night, the animal grows tired of so much comfort and sets out to discover harsher pleasures, more akin to her feline nature, by joining a pack of wild cats, veritable beasts, prowling in the nearby woods. She escapes out of the mere desire to savor the barbaric experience of living in the jungle. Her owner didn't miss her particularly. And one day, sometime later, when she'd forgotten about her, she discovered her in the vicinity of the garden, transformed into a hungry, hirsute, and distrustful little beast. The old woman entices her with delicacies to make her return home. She has the impression that the cat recognizes her old home; indeed, when she steps through the doorway, she again feels that this is the place where she truly belongs. She greedily devours the dishes served to her in the kitchen. Her domesticity is pure fiction. As soon as her appetite is satisfied, she escapes back into the forest to join the violent horde to which she now belongs. The bitter whiff of viscera has suddenly violated that funereal sanctuary. An acrid stench of viscera has violated the enclosure from which life had long since escaped. For Pulkheria Ivanovna, the blow is definitive. She considers the visit and subsequent escape of her former companion as a funereal omen, the unmistakable announcement of an approaching death. And indeed, as Marietta Karapetiz argued, absent any rational explanation from the author to illuminate this fact, the Grim Reaper soon arrives to destroy the oasis where the dead couple played day after day at being alive. A clear case of the triumph of Eros over death."

"Licenciado, you've learned the lesson by heart!" exclaimed Amelia.

Dante de la Estrella stared at her with a mixture of repulsion and perplexity, then looked around at everyone present with an air of consternation, as if coming out of a trance. He took a crumpled handkerchief from his pocket and wiped it over his increasingly reddened face.

"Did the cat go back to live with the old man after they did away with his wife?" asked Juan Ramón.

"It's impossible, my boy, for you to understand, at your age, that life isn't a game. No, it's not. It took me ten years to refute that thesis and its remarkably elementary erotic symbolism," said Dante de la Estrella with a new, velvety, almost wistful voice, puckering his mouth as he spoke until it formed an orifice like that of a hen's ass. "I titled my article 'Does the Lion Believe that Everyone Shares His Condition?' That evening, however, it would have been impossible for me to offer any point of view. It was the first time I'd heard of the Russian author who roused the speaker's passion. It took me a decade of arduous study to master the subject. I became immersed in Gogol. I studied his bibliography. Through the Secretariat, I began to locate and acquire a number of books and journal subscriptions without spending a cent. I had to start from zero. What a challenge! It took time, but I emerged victorious. They didn't pay me anything, but they didn't charge me for publishing the article either, which in itself was a victory. There, in that first text, I put forward my thesis that Gogol had conceived his literature from its beginning as a weapon to achieve national regeneration. By abandoning the traditional ways of storytelling, he was centuries ahead of his time. He made use of an esperpentic world, incoherent nightmares, masks, and every kind of eccentricity as a mere decoy to convey a message, not so much evangelical, as she sometimes, in her naïve confusion, believed, but rather in keeping with the principles of a practical morality. The idyllic world of the old-world landowners was doomed to disappear, not for social or political reasons, as the liberal intransigents wanted; nor could it continue forever and ever to be as it was, as longed for by the apostles of tradition. The problem was different, and on a scale that his contemporaries could not grasp. The sin of Afanasy Ivanovich and Pulkheria Ivanovna lies for me in their absurd and wasteful extravagance, in a visceral inability to envisage economic health, thrift. Such irresponsible minds make it impossible to defend the essence of property. They interrupt progress. Their life is a mere metaphor for waste. They spend a fortune on food and on the maintenance of a legion of servants whose number they don't even know. Their hands aren't made for keeping, but for letting everything go. Do they even know what's grown in their fields? What is the state of their forests? Gogol obliquely condemns the administrative irresponsibility of his landowners and the laziness and malice of their servants, just as in the celebrated story 'The Overcoat' he scornfully chastises the poor devil, the modest clerk, the perfect nobody who doesn't resign himself to conform to his real situation but aspires to a fur-lined coat whose acquisition is far beyond his means. An advanced society can only be reached through austerity and thrift. Gogol should be the bedside author of the contemporary entrepreneur. In my essay, I conceived Pulkheria Ivanovna's rebellious cat as a symbol of the anarchic employee, unionized or not, of our times, capable of doing away with his employer, who, instead of using firmness with him, tries to win his loyalty and understanding with soft philanthropies. These are not gratuitous cruelties. The wage-earner of today, like the wage-earner of all times, I know, is an innocent orphan lost in a world he doesn't know, where everything threatens him. The greatest enemy he has is not his employer, nor the foreman, but his instincts. He fears them more than the devil because he glimpses the power of destruction they bring. Giving them friendship and affection is tantamount to throwing gasoline on a fire whose destiny, obviously, is fulfilled by razing everything to the ground. By turning the world into ashes, the fire is eventually extinguished. The worker knows this. He senses that his thirst for destruction, his instinct, will only be quenched when he has finished with the last log, which is himself. From the depths of his soul rises a clamor that demands order, discipline, an iron hand. In this way the social pact fulfills its mission: harmony. There has never been a society that prospers with caresses other than those of the whip. Only in this way will the smokestacks flourish, will commerce develop, will knowledge prosper, and will well-being and wealth be spread among all layers of society. I pride myself on being the only one of the great Russian author's exegetes who's glimpsed this contemporary vein in his work. When I gather my writings together, I will show an unknown Gogol, an author whom no one, I'm sure, has suspected. I haven't yet done so; my purpose has consisted, above all, in preventing that horrific charlatan from Istanbul from continuing to spread her fallacies. It may seem naïve to you, but I intended to reform her. That's why I sent her and her confederate Rodrigo Vives copies of my articles. But it wasn't I who managed to tame that divine heron, but death. I learned the news from a Canadian journal of Slavic studies. It was a rude shock, I can tell you. From then on, I stopped writing, although I'm convinced that I mustn't forgo publishing my book someday. If there is one thing I am sure of, it is that my convictions have a value in and of themselves, regardless of the theses they refute. The time will come when I'll be able to devote myself completely to my studies. Now that my family spends almost all of its time in Matamoros, perhaps I'll be able to sort everything out. My daughter, as it were, is a quiet woman; as for my son-in-law I barely know his voice. Whereas my wife! The negativity she displays by the mere fact of being anywhere, even if she keeps her lips closed, isn't to be believed. Never mind! The day will come when I'll publish my book, even if my family monster tries to annihilate me with her sulfurous breath. I must begin by tidying up my papers, revising them, supplementing them. I'll eliminate unnecessary reiterations, certain less-than-gallant comments concerning the personality of the deceased. The day will come when my name will begin to ascend as that of the poor Karapetiz slides into oblivion. My spirit will rise toward the supreme light; hers will disintegrate little by little in the hell where she surely dwells." He moved his hands frantically in front of his eyes as if he wished to shake off some unwelcome vision, and a moment later he began to clap his hands with a thunderous enthusiasm whose connection no one understood. When he recovered from this rapture of enthusiasm, fearful that one of those present would wrest the floor away from him, he returned to his topic: "Yes, ladies and gentlemen, at that time, and I admit it again without hesitation, at that dinner on the shores of the Sea of Marmara, I was in no condition to face such a she-wolf; my concerns were of another order. She gave her interpretation of the old, idle pair of landowners and the cat who chose a life in the wild, addressing only Ramona, as if I were not present, but when the final phase came in which she tried to identify the cat with an incarnation of the life-giving animal impulse, Eros, libido, or some twaddle or the other, she stared at me piercingly. Her eyes seemed to want to drill into my already exhausted brain. By this time, my fury had completely dissipated. I was, on the other hand, terrified, I must confess. The woman at that moment caused me an unassailable fear and repulsion. Behind the elegant black moiré dress that imprisoned her flesh, behind her silver necklaces and rings, behind her perfect makeup, I imagined a huge and dissolute cat, ready to run away with the Gypsies of the orchestra, with the smugglers of the most dangerous of ports, with a gang of thugs from the worst neighborhoods of Palermo. She also gave off an odor of wild substances that intoxicated and intimidated those around her. She seemed to read my thoughts. Her gaze, already cruel when fixed on me, suddenly displayed a fierce feline gleam. 'The simulacra of life,' she said, when at last she deigned to address me, 'come at a very high price. Know it, Ciriaco, know it well. Cultivating forces hostile to life usually produces very bitter fruits.' She let out a metallic guffaw. It seemed as if an invisible hand were moving the jaws of a skull from the inside to cause her to emit that bristly and invective laugh. Crack, crack, crack, crack, crack! I attempted to say something, but before I could think of the words, she'd already turned to Ramona: 'Forgive me, my dear, forgive me! I, your humble servant, am hopeless. I must have put you to sleep with my boring little lecture. When you see me monopolizing the conversation, feel free to stop me. Be good. Knock me on the head with your fists if necessary. Hit me over the head, I beg you. That's all this not-always-submissive Mexican woman who lived at Calle de la Palma, number ninety-five, apartment seven asks of you . . . Ramoncita, child, be merciful and forgive all the useless palavering from this sassy old broad who still doesn't realize that she's no longer the divine heron that one day she was made to believe she was.'"

Of all the members of the Millares family, none surpassed the twins in their attention to and enjoyment of the spectacle offered by Dante de la Estrella. Juan Ramón took advantage of the pause to ask:

"Could that woman really turn herself into a cat?"

"I'm certain of it, a cat, a panther, or something worse. Much worse. I won't go into details out of respect for you. No one reveres the innocence of children more than I. My wife is the mother of two daughters who were once your noble and tender age. One died; the other, now married, lives with her family in Matamoros. I hope they stay there for the rest of their lives! But, I assure you, that woman could turn herself into something worse than a cat. Next to her, a hyena would have seemed like a very sweet animal. By that time, Ramona had already taken out, like the model pupil she believed herself to be, a little notebook the color of her dress and a very sophisticated gold Parker pen and wrote down with disgusting servility everything that Marietta Karapetiz, swollen with pride, slowly reeled out, like the President of the Republic at the moment he dictates to his secretary the text of a decree of paramount importance. She was no longer the anteater, the opossum rooting around and among the dishes; she'd become once again the toucan, proud of her powerful beak, awaiting an occasion to launch her treacherous attack. With the attitude and voice of a stateswoman, the Professor continued to talk about Gogol, about his eccentricities, the legends that circulated during his lifetime, rumors spread by his enemies, terrible, very grave accusations, including that of necrophilia; she spoke about 'Evenings Near the Village of Dikanka,' a text she described as decisive for having at least glimpsed the psychological complexity, the labyrinth in which that damaged and anguished sexuality was lost. I fixed that conversation in my memory. I rejected, corrected, and sorted out everything in my articles, of which, as I've already said, I sent copies to the interested party and to that resounding nothing that life saw fit to turn Rodrigo Vives into."

A lightning bolt flashed across the mountain, followed by a

string of thunderclaps. Each one seemed to be an expanded echo of the previous one. Dante C. de la Estrella jumped to his feet startled, let out a scream, and fell back onto the sofa. He appeared to have suffered a conniption. The only thing that moved was his mouth, which opened and closed nonstop between intermittent gasps.

V

Wherein the attorney in question, without setting out to, manages to tame the Divine Heron, and the general mirth that follows his victory is magnified by the sudden appearance of the cheerful Sacha.

ONLY THE TWINS REMAINED IN place, in front of their puzzles, apparently unfazed by the Licenciado's fainting spell. The adults, on the other hand, immediately sprang into action. Amelia ran to the kitchen. The Millares men, father and son, approached the fallen man cautiously. Don Antonio began to feel for a pulse; at that moment the moaning and contortions ceased. Dante de la Estrella opened his eyes and observed, with genuine stupefaction, the behavior of the others.

"Can you explain to me what sort of joke this is?" he demanded. From just his bloodshot cheeks and neck and the swelling of his eyelids, it was obvious that something abnormal had just happened to him.

"We wanted to know how your blood pressure was," said Amelia, who reappeared with a pitcher of water.

"My blood pressure? Both my blood pressure and my health in general are nobody's business but my own." De la Estrella seemed not to have been aware that he fainted, nor could he figure out what had happened. He understood only that something had escaped him. With a sudden expression of alarm, he put his hand to his chest, made sure that his wallet was still in the inside pocket of his jacket, and seemed reassured that it was. He resumed the story at the exact point where he'd left off. "By this time, both women had managed to exclude me entirely from the conversation. Dignity prevented me from noticing, much less protesting. I went back to eating, to drinking, to ordering more food. I've never had problems with my blood pressure, Millares! Whoever told you that is a charlatan. They're everywhere! I guess that Marietta Karapetiz was afraid I might finish off her portions, because suddenly she paused and counseled Ramona: 'Look, my dear, while you all are in Istanbul, we'll have new opportunities to return to these subjects, if you are really interested in them. I suggest you pay tribute to Elagabalus before our voracious Ciriaco finishes everything off.' That malicious comment could have been the straw that broke an already overburdened camel's back. However, I closed my eyes, took a very deep breath, counted to thirty-five, out loud to make sure I was heard, and forced myself to smile. The smile must have been somewhat forced, as I felt an excruciating tightness in my gums, my cheekbones, my upper lip, even the corners of my mouth. However, I can say that I managed to keep my cool. 'Excuse me, señora, perhaps because we were introduced so hastily you weren't able to catch my name correctly. It often happens, I'm aware of it, but to understand all is to forgive all, since the natural decay inflicted by the years, and the submission, like it or not, to the whims of the jubilant but irresponsible Bacchus, tend to lead to this kind of misunderstanding. You have pronounced my name incorrectly on several occasions. My name is Dante de la Estrella.' 'Dante C. de la Estrella,' she replied with marked sarcasm, and added: 'Dante Ciriaco de la Estrella, to serve God and the world! Do you see how I didn't forget it? Stop worrying about such trifles, my dear. At my age, any name is difficult to remember; at times, I won't deny, I get lost, I get confused; my ear is no longer what it used to be when I was, yes, myself, don't laugh, I, your attentive and assured servant, a delicious little *güerita*, harassed by a horny louse, with domicile in the Mexican capital on the centrally located Calle de La Palma . . .'"

"Number ninety-five, apartment seven!" exclaimed the twins in unison.

"That's right," grumbled the Licenciado in evident bad humor; and he repeated: "'With domicile in the Mexican capital, in the centrally located Calle de La Palma, number ninety-five, apartment seven, Humbly Yours, the residence, lest anyone think otherwise; I don't wish any misinterpretations, nor give the impression that I'm looking for someone to take liberties with me. Nothing of the sort! Respect! Do you understand me? Respect!' She laughed in my face with scoffing malice. What would you have advised me to do at that point, Millares?" A purely rhetorical question, because before the architect could open his mouth, the narrator, as usual, had already retaken the floor. "Get up from the table, take a cab and leave Ramona alone with that permanent fountain of provocations? What to do? The eternal question of decisive moments! What to do? Tell them both to go to hell or continue to suffer all manner of insults like a blithering idiot?"

"Was there no way to convince Ramona Vives to return with you to the hotel?" asked old man Millares.

"None! It's obvious that you don't know that woman. She would have spit in my eye, I'm certain. By that time, at Marietta Karapetiz's request, the musicians had returned to our table.

She ordered something in Turkish and the band started to play 'Ramona,' that old song that's an eternal favorite of the sappy people of this world. You should have seen the violinist, twisting like a cripple sandwiched in between that unbearable pair of women! The Professor crooned a few words in Spanish: '*Ramoooona, gentil artista de mi amoooor,*' and added others in Italian, and still others in a language unknown to me. At the end of the performance, the women applauded wildly. Marietta Karapetiz dismissed the musicians with one of those quick, dry, autocratic gestures in which she seemed to have earned her doctorate, and they withdrew, bowing deeply. She seemed to feel obliged to explain to us the cause of her sharp dismissal. 'Ramona' had to sparkle like a flawless diamond; its sparkle could not be dimmed by other songs; otherwise it would be just another tune, trivial, bland. That was all. She took off one of her rings and placed it on one of Ramona's fingers. 'It will bring you much luck. It's antique silver from Turkmenia. A ritual object, almost impossible to find for sale. You can only buy it in the Bazaar of Ashgabat. And not always for money, but through barter or as payment for a service. It was there that the indefatigable and prodigious Karapetiz acquired it for me.' The likewise indefatigable but never prodigious Ramona again opened her little red notebook and recorded diligently the name of the place and its characteristics. '*Ashgabat, capital of Turkmenia, on the border with ancient Persia, that is, present-day Iran.*' 'You can also write down, my Angel of Light, that the bazaar is in the middle of the desert, not far from the capital. An open-air bazaar, with no roof save the sky. The best time to shop is in the early hours of the morning. Make a note, because this is important: after nine o'clock there is little or nothing to see. One begins to wander about in the midst of a crimson fog that dazes and almost blinds. A man walks about as if

sleepwalking. The desert is draped with carpets whose red rever-
berates beneath the glow of a crazed sun that extracts the color of
the fabrics and causes it to float at eye level. The camels themselves
get dizzy, writhe, vomit, and what can I say of us humans? I would
like to see our Ciriaco in those godforsaken places! At one end
of that immense carpet of wool and silk that the desert suddenly
becomes, the vendors of other products are grouped together,
forming geometric designs. Those selling jewelry are placed next
to each other, until they form a waning moon, the moon of Islam.
These are shapes that date back many centuries. The women stand
with their arms outstretched, from which they hang silver belts,
brooches, armlets, and bracelets; the squatting men watch over
them. Those who sell cheese and curdled milk form the points of a
star; in the end, what does it matter to us, am I not right? At home
I have all the documents that Karapetiz collected about that fabulous market. One of his first studies! You'll see, *Ramooona, gentil
artista de mi amooor,* how many surprises I've prepared at home for
you and your brother.' At this point I was more than bored of hearing all this rubbish. I was annoyed, fed up, above all, that those two
Miss Know-It-Alls, who in my opinion were beginning to treat each
other with excessive and suspicious intimacy, insisted on declaring
me nonexistent, and that the few times they seemed to notice me
they did so with belittling names, so I decided to interrupt their
cloying conversation unexpectedly. It was a surprise attack, a tactic
whose effectiveness in disorienting the enemy I'd already proved.
I filled a glass of wine to the brim and downed it in one gulp. It's
impossible to know how many I'd already finished off at that point!
'I'd be interested to know what class of people are here tonight,'
I suddenly exclaimed, in a voice perhaps louder than was necessary, driven by the sheer need to exist that had incubated during

the long time I'd spent as a ghost. Both women pretended to be startled; they stared at me with a most offensive attitude of calculated surprise. 'What is it that you actually mean to ask Professor Karapetiz?' inquired Ramona, in her most fragrant voice of a pupil of the Sagrado Corazón de Jesús, spilling onto the table a repulsive aroma of false tenderness. 'What you heard was as simple as that! I want to know what class of people frequent this restaurant!' I repeated in a voice that pierced my eardrum. 'But what is this man talking about? Is there anyone who understands him? What class of people? What does he mean by that?' asked Marietta Karapetiz, her eyebrows raised in astonishment. 'Exactly that! What class of people are around us?' I squawked on the verge of collapse. 'Class? In what sense do you employ that word?' she asked with perfect, icy, cruel, patient, unflappable politeness. And there my doltish compatriot intervened again: 'Couldn't you be more explicit, Dante Ciriaco?' There it was again, hounding with that name they wouldn't let go of! 'When you speak of class, do you mean it in the sociological sense of the term? Are you interested in knowing if the restaurant's clientele is made up of workers, peasants, middle class, or members of the bourgeoisie? Speak up, is that what you mean?' I couldn't take it anymore, who could! I howled, 'Look, Dumbona, the only thing I did was ask what class of people usually dine here. Is that too inaccessible for your level of comprehension?' 'So now it's clear! Come now, my boy, just by asking such a foolish question, you're complicating things a lot!' the old Professor said after a sigh of martyrdom, as if she'd just invented the wheel. 'Look, the customers are mostly Turks, which is only natural, or are you going to complain about that too, although some foreigners also come here, not so much tourists, who spoil everything, but Istanbul residents, businessmen, consular officials, what do I know! No one has ever asked me such a question before! Cultivated people come here, I dare say, although at times some schlub without a tie slips in,' she fixed her gaze on my neck. Blood rushed to my face. 'An occupational hazard, in any restaurant, I imagine. Look how impeccably dressed everyone is. I suppose they're attracted to this place by the good food, a certain discreet elegance, nothing pompous, and, of course, the music, which is excellent. I may be wrong, and in that case, you'll have to excuse me, but I don't dare go to the tables to disturb the guests, to interrogate them,' and she added a few words that I barely understood: 'I'm not a nightingale, but in my trills, I've sometimes managed to reach a high C.' I couldn't take it anymore. I tried to keep my voice from shaking and barely managed to articulate: 'Cultivated people? Are you sure about what you're saying? Perhaps you're the only one who thinks so. Some people are more charitable than others in judging their neighbor, and it seems to me that you, out of generosity, or lack of worldliness, are guilty of being too permissive. I assure you that in the short time we've been here I've seen a lady or two, and in this regard my intuition rarely fails me, who'd like to take it up the ass.' '¡Olé, torero!' the unpredictable widow Karapetiz responded in a raucous cry."

The twins burst out laughing. The others joined in.

"Well, well, well! What conversations you had with that very peculiar lady!" Amelia commented. "Children, I think it's about time you put away your things so you can start setting the table!"

"I beg your forgiveness a thousand times, señora! I implore you to pardon the many ramblings that have flowed from my lips on this unpleasant stormy evening. How many years did you work with me, Millares? Twelve? Fifteen? Did you ever hear me say anything like that? Never! This sailor's language doesn't suit me at all. That night in Istanbul I was the first to be surprised to hear myself use such shocking language. A phrase born of the pure necessity to confuse the enemy, I swear. The comment shot out of my mouth in the most natural way in the world. It came from my irrational side, from my nocturnal side. I urgently needed to undo the alliance that those two women had formed against me. To derail, more than anything else, the composure of that imperious harpy, to punish her dreadful arrogance. After all, was I or was I not a human being? You must understand, the only thing I sought to do was to get out of the corner where I was confined and where, truth be told, I was suffocating. To show the world that Dante de la Estrella, no matter how obscure he might seem to certain divas, existed. The result was more than surprising. First that thunderous '*¡Olé, torero!*' which must have been heard as far as the kitchen of the restaurant across the street. The two imposing rows of teeth turned toward me, suddenly devoid of their usual ferocity; what's more, with a smile of open complicity. Ramona seemed distraught. Upon hearing my elaboration on the desires prized by certain local ladies she'd even hiccupped. But when she saw Marietta Karapetiz's reaction, she ventured a vague smile, and held onto it out of pure commitment, keeping her distance from me, which by then was already chasmic. The tyrant continued her harangue. 'Pure Mexican from head to toe! From the very Highlands of Jalisco, I could swear it! Dearest, I know that sublime and pestilential clay, swelling with creative imagination, mixed with the same ethereal substance that dreams are made of! How many times have I knelt before that sacred clay to grasp a sliver of light!'"

If, moments before, the Licenciado De la Estrella had frightened the Millares family by suffering a fainting spell, the feverish gesticulation he displayed at that moment in order to reproduce the unrestrained flow of the frenzied Señora De Karapetiz, the imitation of her gestures, the incoherence of her expression, the shouts, sighs, and laments troubled them even more. He opened and closed his eyes nonstop, rolled them in their sockets, squinted; his lips seemed to have turned to rubber, so unusual were their movements. None of his muscles were able to remain still for a second; his hands spun wildly, like blades that had become detached from a windmill. The words gushed out, colliding, one against the other, choking the speaker, turning his face purple. Everything in him was rushing toward total convulsion. The spectacle adopted an almost repulsive quality. Old man Millares got up, poured himself a brandy, and offered one to the Licenciado, who refused with a gesture.

"Perhaps a whiskey, better yet a coffee . . . ," Don Antonio insisted.

"No, no, no, no! But I'll ask for one if I need it, or, in any case, I'll pour it myself. Please don't interrupt me now." He took out a large, brightly colored handkerchief, dabbed his face, and then continued, "I didn't have an idea what that woman was talking about. Her soliloquy went on for a good while: 'The great Constantine Porphyrogenitus was an intuitive, a sublime visionary. But in this city a wise man, after years of laborious inquiry, can only sketch an idea; on the other hand, in his country, which is also mine— I'm not a chinaca, poblana, tehuana, jarocha for nothing—the people themselves, from the patricians to the simplest, most innocent strata, transform an idea with amazing ease into real and everyday events, into flesh of their flesh, daily and most sacred food. Virgen Morena, help this miserable sinner who today implores your protection! Santo Niño del Agro, a thousand times worthy of veneration, unceasing succor to the despondent, absolve me, for I feel myself perishing from pure ecstasy and rejoicing!' I could only think of two possibilities: that she was taunting me with that clamorous fanfaronade, or that she'd gone outright mad. I didn't see a third way. Would I yet be given the opportunity that night to witness the arrival of shrinks and watch the nervous toucan be restrained in a straitjacket? Marietta Karapetiz paused, poured herself a glass of water, and drank in a single gulp the contents along with two yellowish tablets. 'You will forgive me, little ones, this slight digression. When I get together with Mexicans a moment always comes when I imagine I'm back there, in the country where I felt like a fish in water. I grew up in a village in the south of the New World. Yes, my friend, your language is also my first language, in case you hadn't guessed,' she said, with a look that suggested lingering defiance, which, fortunately, faded almost immediately. 'Are you satisfied? Do you know everything about me now? Don't believe it; you know even less. I arrived at that town with my parents in 1905. I was very young. I was born into one world and grew up in a completely different one. I thought I was happy, even though I sensed that something was missing that I couldn't pinpoint. It was only when I set foot in Mexico that I discovered my soul. I love Mexicans. No one in the world is as generous as they. They adored me. To the point of making me feel like a divine heron. The Divine Heron wrapped up in a bow! Nothing less! That was me, a not-at-all-ugly girl beginning to make her way in life. Sometimes that counts. I'd recently married the hardworking Karapetiz. It was my first trip by sea. As the ship approached Veracruz, what impressed me most was how the sky changed colors. For a couple of days all we'd seen was the whiteness of the seagulls. Suddenly it seemed that the birds changed color and behavior. The zopilote appeared, the Caribbean cousin of the vulture. I'd never seen it, but its fierce personality, its unyielding discretion, and its many other virtues commanded my respect from the very first moment. It's true, I'd never seen those birds with their black plumage and gangrenous necks before. They began to approach the ship with complete confidence, to perch on its masts and ropes, to walk on deck, to the horror, I must say, of some fainthearted passengers, with the bouncing, lethargic trot of aging knights returning from some new adventure. At port I noticed that the city belonged to them. The people would come out into the streets to throw rotting meat at them, and they crowded together, elated to take part in that unexpected repast. Such banquets aren't always a model of harmony. I remember seeing a little girl of about eleven or twelve years old walking along, her little brother in one hand and a chamber pot in the other. I saw her empty the basin on the sidewalk, a step away from us. What tremendous joy! What an Olympic feast! Like the ancient Spartans, those animals knew how to link the pleasures of the table with those of battle. A veritable flower war took place before my eyes! With bloodied necks and legs, some with a missing eye, all of them more or less plucked, the survivors celebrated their triumph gleefully by tasting those morsels of ambrosia. More arrived, and in a matter of seconds they bore witness to the corpses of the vanquished. An insignificant pile of bones, a few feathers scattered on the breeze, and the city regained, as if by magic, its traditional cleanliness!' At that point she stopped her picturesque as well as implausible recollections. She turned to me with a radiant smile that allowed her to display her entire, and extraordinary, set of teeth that looked like old, polished ivory. And with the same smile, which suggested nothing but friendship, she shot point-blank: 'So tell me, my dear, what do you think the ladies around us would like to do?' She asked the question so out of the blue that I was left speechless. I had already said it; I had thought that my

outburst, due to its vulgar provocation, was going to offend her. It'd
been a way to protect myself, perhaps even to exact revenge, from
the deluge of hoodoo I'd suffered through during the course of the
night. The effect, however, was completely unexpected: a sudden
amour fou, a string of phrases tossed to the wind, all of them incomprehensible to me. A dizziness of the soul, a loss of reason. I don't
know what they were. And when I was most defenseless, she was
overcome, on a whim, to hear again the vulgarity I'd uttered a short
time before. I wasn't very amused by the matter. Just as it had gone
well by chance, repeating it could have fatal results. She insisted:
'Say those little words again. Repeat them. Be generous. You don't
know how amusing I found them. My goodness, what beautiful
lips you have!' she said, running her fingers over my mouth, 'but
even more beautiful are the words they're able to speak!' From the
ashes where she'd been lying half buried all this while, our national
Ramona was resurrected at the wrong time. All night long I'd
endured her looks full of maliciousness, acrimony, and mounting
resentment. At that moment she was dying of envy. And jealousy.
I also imagine that spiritually she must have been somewhat lost,
trying to find her bearings in a terrain that was certainly alien to
her; not unlike me, on the other hand. 'You're all grown up now,'
she pressed, 'and yet you choose to act like a baby. Repeat what
you said. Show some maturity. Go on, what are you waiting for?'
Who better than you, Millares, could sympathize with my bewilderment! I commented, but without attaching any importance to
my words, that, by pure intuition and a precocious knowledge of
life, I'd come to believe that some of the ladies present wouldn't
be opposed to indulging that night in rather perverse pleasures
and performing certain practices that, strictly speaking, were to be
considered against nature. Marietta Karapetiz didn't allow me to

continue. 'No, no, no, no, and no!' she shouted. 'Don't be a coward! Why don't you repeat what you said? Or are you afraid?' I continued to refuse, although my embarrassment began to give way; I understood that by doing so I could become the master of the situation. And by taking that path I could tame the divine heron. She ended up proclaiming at the top of her lungs: 'You assured everyone that almost all the females here are dripping like bitches in heat for someone to churn butter in their asses tonight.' And once again she repeated the expression that she apparently resorts to in such circumstances, '¡Olé, torero!' amid fits of laughter and unbridled applause. Then from the other tables, here and there, like an echo, we heard shouts of: '¡Olé, torero!' '¡Olé, torero!'"

The twins burst out laughing again. A sigh from Amelia expressed that she was no longer amused by the presence of her niece at that gathering.

"I beg your pardon, señora, allow me to offer a thousand and one apologies! Forgive me, Millares!" he continued. "I apologize for the language that that woman was accustomed to using. My only aim is to remain faithful to the facts. I'm convinced that if one begins to falsify the small story, the big one, that of the Universe, would become debased to the point of turning into a tangled, incomprehensible mess. I was scandalized by her brazenness, which far surpassed that of my comment." De la Estrella seemed to settle down. He remained in a limbo of pedantic gluttony, admiring, it seemed, his own expository ability. "I continued to study with the greatest attention the two women at my table. The old woman was, as I have already said, a toucan with the pretensions of a Grandee of Spain, a collection of dark, massive flesh. The other, some thirty years younger, vague and watery like a soft-boiled egg, was her antithesis. Although not fat, she looked as if she were about to spill over onto the table. Everything on Marietta Karapetiz's face was closed, tawny, hard; there was nothing in Ramona Vives's face that wasn't formless, blurred; the garish makeup on her characterless face looked as if it had been mixed with the cotton candy that they sell at carnivals. One had large, wide, almond-shaped eyes, a shade that resembled a bright, greenish honey, the other's were round, like a pair of dull, wistful, black buttons. The hair tightly pulled toward the nape of Karapetiz's neck was as black as a raven's wing; that of my compatriot was ashen, a cluster of a thousand tiny curls and ringlets that covered part of her forehead, further accentuating her doll-like inexpressiveness. The old woman's teeth were strong, savage, as if carved from lightly weathered ivory; those of the poor Señorita Vives were of all sizes, and they were stacked one on top of the other, like scraps of bones pieced together with absolute randomness. Nevertheless, despite these and various other differences between teacher and disciple, they'd established, it seems to me, from the beginning, powerful currents of integration, such that one tended to think that both women belonged to the same family."

"And were there ties of that sort? Were they related in any way?"

"I'm referring, señora, to the fact that they belonged to the same spiritual family," the Licenciado cut her off with bitter formality. "I have taken the liberty of expressing myself in similes. The very existence of men, their passions, longings, downfalls, and hopes, has been considered by much greater thinkers than I, your humble servant, as a mere metaphor for the Universe."

Salvador Millares was unable to contain a belly laugh.

"Have I, perhaps without realizing it, resorted to some comedic effect? Have I said anything that might incite laughter?"

"Nothing in particular," answered the architect, without losing his sense of humor, "but as far as I can tell, Licenciado, there is something that scares you and keeps you from finishing the story. You speed up then slow down. You move ahead a bit and then go backward almost immediately. What could be the reason?"

"You'll find out soon enough. And you'll see how little comedy there is in what happened to me on the trip. None! On the contrary. Look, my reflections on the physical differences of my tablemates and their psychological resemblance aren't gratuitous. They don't serve as mere decoration in this tale, rather they fulfill a structural need of the story. In a way they exemplify my disaffection, my defenselessness, the barrenness of my effort. How could I pretend to tame a woman, who to make matters worse believed she was the divine heron, when each new situation required that I repeat all my efforts and start from zero? We belonged to different, antagonistic, spiritual families. On the other hand, at every turn they found *vases* that connected and strengthened them . . . But, anyway, where were we?"

"In Istanbul."

"Thank you, that's very kind of you; I assure you I've not forgotten," he said sarcastically. "What I'm asking is where I left off."

"The Professor frequently made chronological mistakes," Don Antonio ventured.

"That's what I was talking about? Chronological mistakes? For what purpose? Ah, I get it! Of course! We'd already moved on to other things, but I can use that point to start over. It wasn't that Marietta Karapetiz often made mistakes; she did it constantly. She moved through time with absolute disregard. She established chronologies that were entirely personal. Even I, who do not consider myself at all a specialist in my country's past, was able to detect that when she referred to certain historical figures, she placed them in periods in which they in no way belonged. At times she turned everything into a grotesque caricature. Perhaps, I thought, it was because she and her husband had traveled to Mexico on different occasions between 1908 and 1926. Sometimes their stays were long, others minimal. On a trip that coincided with Obregón's assassination, they stayed a mere four days, a ridiculous length of time considering the duration of the sea voyage in those days. It was almost normal that in such circumstances memories would become confused. Later I observed that the same was true with her references to geography. She mingled and confused areas that had no relationship whatsoever. Most of Karapetiz's research was limited to southern and southeastern Mexico. In speaking of her travels through Yucatán, Tabasco, Chiapas, and Oaxaca, she cited the delightful days she'd spent in Colima and the discovery of Guanajuato and Taxco. On one occasion they were traveling from Mérida to Campeche and were ecstatic to contemplate Zacatecas's red walls, bathed in the light of dawn. I began to wonder whether her knowledge of Gogol, of which she'd made such a big display at the beginning of the evening, might also suffer from the same flight of fancy, the same radical lack of rigor. At times that woman gave the impression of never having been to Mexico, of basing her knowledge on poorly remembered films, postcards, second- or thirdhand accounts, of being the product of unrelated readings. Despite this, her exploits took on a fantastic dimension thanks to her extraordinary mastery of storytelling. I must say, and I don't apologize for acknowledging it, that the quality of the story, its effects, its brilliance, its intensity, made the most absurd circumstances plausible and much more attractive than the descriptions from archaeologists, ethnographers, and explorers tend to be. I began to listen to her and suddenly I was bewitched, yes, I assure you, bewitched in the strictest sense of the word, as if I'd been subjected to an act of hypnosis. To say nothing of Ramona. She hung, as they say, on her every word and jotted them down in her notebook at an astonishing speed. Through that woman's voice, the witch doctors and healers of Chiapas and Veracruz began to transform into Siberian shamans, into amazing sorcerers from the heart of Africa, into visionary monks from Tibetan monasteries. Her culture was spectacular. And she was a born actress. One could listen to her without blinking for hours on end, I swear. Even her language became more refined, free of ribald flummery, vulgar populism—¡*Olé, torero! ¡Olé, torero! ¡Olé, torero!*—that had adorned it in frequent moments of excitement. Now, I repeat, I don't have the slightest certainty of the veracity of her assertions, but I am certain, after studying some of her writings in depth, that we were dealing with a case of flimflam second to none. Marietta Karapetiz was an impostor in the flesh. I doubt she ever . . . Well, I don't want to get ahead of myself. I can't remember at what point in the evening's spectacle the extraordinary woman riveted her gaze on the door. Her eyes lit up; her teeth gleamed. A ferocious she-wolf proud to show off her cub! 'But my little white dove has arrived!' she cried. I turned my head; a smiling old man with a swarthy face and brilliant white hair, in an elegant white linen suit, was approaching our table, leaning on an ivory-colored cane with a black handle. His teeth, like Marietta's, didn't seem to fit in his mouth. His eyes were large, round, very expressive; they were cheerful and playful eyes, like those of a puppy, a very pale blue, which contrasted with his dark skin and accentuated his distinguished air even more. I was able to see that he was moving one leg with noticeable effort; the right one, it seemed. He arrived, rested his hands on our table, and, before greeting or introducing himself, insinuated a dazzling smile, only to then immediately recite in a deep voice the following shocking stanza:

"'Whether I shit hard or shit soft,
in the light or in the dark,
be my patron, I implore,
little Saint whom I adore!'"

The whole Millares family burst out laughing.

"'No, Sacha, no! This time we've really made a mistake,' she shouted. The old man, puzzled, looked at us one by one, waiting for an explanation. 'This gentleman, whom you see sitting with us with such nobility,' she explained, 'isn't Rodrigo Vives. Sit down, please, and have a glass of wine with us. You've probably had dinner, haven't you, my little dove?' and she made the introductions: 'My brother Alexander, my great, my only true friend; Señorita Ramona Vives, sister of the illustrious Rodrigo of the same surname; Licenciado Dante C. de la Estrella, his real name, as incredible as it may seem, who's accompanying the Vives siblings on their trip to Turkey.' She insisted again, 'Have you been struck mute? Have you eaten supper?' And again, without allowing him to answer, she offered an explanation about the crass recitation her brother had delivered. It was the fragment of a supplication to a little holy boy, truly miraculous, whose devotion enjoyed immense fervor in certain regions of Mexico during the first two decades of the century. 'My husband studied and documented the cult, and he, my very own holy boy, wanted to surprise Rodrigo, who is especially interested in Karapetiz's notes on this phenomenon.' 'Could you repeat the verses?' asked the insatiable little shit, Ramoncita.

"'Little turd, come out,
out of your spout!'"

The cackles from the twins and their grandfather interrupted the story again.

"As you may have noticed, I was living in the extremes of a dream. I was moving among the highest peaks, but also the abysses of thought. Between splendor and dross! Radical points, whose proximity could have dizzied anyone not as strong as I. I felt steady even though I'd imbibed a spectacular amount by that time. Marietta Karapetiz commented that the prayer wasn't worth writing down, that she had all the materials ready, the precious Santo Niño prayer card, the exhaustive comments of the fastidious Karapetiz. 'Your brother is going to be dazzled by the richness of the files, their history, their interpretation. The papers will reveal my husband's high intellectual distinction. I have the impression that Vives will be able to appreciate them. They go from substance to concept, movement to idleness, the visible to the invisible; that is to say from the dregs to the sacred.' 'How could he not write a precious work,' interjected the brother, 'if all the material he collected for his study was like a bunch of grapes of the finest gold!' I must confess that I couldn't quite get my bearings; once again I felt a little lost. So I simply listened to them. 'To begin with,' it was the sister Karapetiz who spoke now, 'the trip itself was already a feast. Sacha accompanied us; he was still a child, but what delight he took in the festivities! The little fellow was almost crowned king of the feast!' 'Where the earth is hot, celebrations tend to be more enjoyable than those in cold climates,' the newcomer commented in a doctoral tone. 'Very true,' she agreed, and added, almost in a pathos of elation, 'And how well you expressed it, little dove, what depths are hidden in your words! In the torrid zones the element of pleasure is usually more intense, more direct, and at the same time more ambiguous than in the Septentrion, because in the sun the body becomes the protagonist; it plays a double role, as body and as abstraction of the body in the ritual celebration. Ah, what Dionysian moments! So many different currents that flow into the same river! A game of creation and disrobing! The creation of the mask until absolute nudity is achieved, total transparence, a privileged state of tension in which it's no longer necessary to search for a face because we've all become, we are already, The Face!' 'Friends,' Sacha rejoined, 'it was truly a privileged place. Coconut trees here, mango trees there. Luxuriant trees everywhere! The most beautiful imaginable! Everything in that land existed in abundance, animals with a voluptuous gait, perfumed rivers, clouds of herons on one side, parrots on the other. And what colors! I said it then and I still maintain: man was born to contemplate beauty, that infinite variety of orchids and birds, only this can redeem him from all his faults and all his sufferings. What wonder to be there, what great, great wonder!' 'Every year,' the sister continued, 'during the feast, a teenage boy was chosen; he had to meet, of course, certain criteria to be the representative at the next feast of the Santo Niño del Agro, who was being celebrated. One time, the dashing Sacha received almost all the votes. He was a little darling, a real sweetheart. Later you'll see him in the photos with his flowered staff, his little white garland, his pot in his hand. But the vote wasn't in his favor.' 'Look, it takes bad luck! To lose by one vote! By one vote!' the old man's voice ended transformed into a pure lament. 'It was the most important vote, and this Sacha, who in many ways is a man of very limited scope, has never managed to understand. That one vote which he curses so much was cast by none other than the wife of the Cacique of the region. A vote that was worth a million. A nephew of hers was selected. A tremendous injustice! The parishioners were outraged. Anyway, even without the victory, it was the most beautiful feast we've ever attended. The feast of our life! Isn't that right, Sachenka?' They spoke with such fervor, with such manifest nostalgia, that it was touching to hear them. Suddenly we noticed that the restaurant was about to close. Ramona asked for the bill. When the waiter brought it, Sacha hurried to intercept it, and said that we were his guests that night, that he couldn't forget that we came from a country that had treated him, his sister, and his poor brother-in-law, the late Karapetiz, like kings and queens. 'To be treated like a queen means nothing to me,' the widow asserted with a contemptuous gesture. 'A queen! What is a queen today? Queens are a dime a dozen; they even have them at carnivals. The treatment I received was far superior; in Mexico, allow me to say again, I came to believe, to feel that I was a divine heron; from daybreak to very late at night I felt as if I were the Divine Heron wrapped up in a bow.' At that point, the pitiful little student whom I was chaperoning, who apparently knew nothing about good manners, began to act like a mad woman; had she seen the bill as I had, I don't believe she would have prolonged the ridiculous little scandal with which she graced us until the end of the gathering. She insisted that it had been her brother who'd extended the invitation, and that he would not forgive her if she failed to carry out his instructions. She stubbornly repeated that we should be the ones to pay the bill, otherwise she wouldn't get up from the table. 'We?' I said to myself, 'Sure, bitch, where am I going to get that kind of money?' I had to set things straight. With an energetic voice of authority, I shouted that she was behaving with inconceivable boorishness, that she was insulting that elderly gentleman, a friend of Mexico, who, with the highest sense of hospitality, wished to regale us. It was necessary to respect his status as a host because we were in his land, and not to humiliate him as she was so obviously doing. So the great Sacha, who perhaps just out of the love of the gesture had put his hand on the check, was forced to take out his little bills and quietly pay the outrageous amount. 'I hope to soon have the opportunity to reciprocate in Mexico in a deserving fashion,' I said with the theatricality required by those circumstances, while Ramona's eyes sparked in such a way that if she'd been near me, I would've been singed. The siblings didn't allow us to accompany them. We returned by cab to the Pera Palace. I'd said goodbye to my new friends with the greatest cordiality. With hugs, kisses, pats on the back. Marietta Karapetiz placed a hand on mine to say how much she'd enjoyed my conversation. 'Brilliant young man, you have much to give to the world. Go read Gogol, you'll love him; we'll talk some other time. Right now all you need to know is that I expect great, great things from you. You're not finished here; your look is telling me so . . .' I got into the car, moved, almost on the verge of tears, full of respect for that woman, and more so of admiration for the good judgment, the wit, the boldness, the quick response that I'd shown, virtues to which I attributed the transformation of that prickly puss into my friend and confederate. I had tamed the divine heron! And I had ousted Ramona from her place as the sole interlocutor so as to turn her into what she was meant to be: a mere listener, a stooge. The car already in motion, I asked the driver to stop for a moment. I got out, ran to the elderly pair, took Marietta Karapetiz's hand and kissed it once, twice, several times. She said new prodigious things that were like a balm to my ears, accustomed until then to hear nothing but insults or inanities. I commented later in the car on the intelligence, the sympathy, and, above all, the vitality of that pair of siblings. An icy voice answered that fortunately there existed people who were ageless; their inner richness kept them forever young, which would never happen to the mediocre who proliferated in this world. I resented the barb, but I decided to keep quiet. Shortly before arriving at the hotel, I made a last effort to mend fences, explaining to her as calmly as possible why, in all fairness, it was Sacha's place to pay the bill. She replied with a comment so churlish that I prefer not to repeat it. Once at the hotel, I got out of the car and went inside without even saying goodnight, leaving her to deal with the driver as best she could, since she was feeling so munificent! Despite the scene caused by this petty little person, I arrived at my room in a magnificent mood, stretched out on the bed, thanked life for having given me a night like that, unlike any other I'd ever known. I'd dazzled an extraordinary woman, and also Sacha, Alexander, her old holy boy, who, as she said, was a darling, a real sweetheart."

VI

Wherein Dante C. de la Estrella glimpses a past belonging to Professor Karapetiz very different from the one he imagined, relates the personal vicissitudes that led him, despite some resistance on his part, to his hymeneals, and learns of the agony and death of Nikolai V. Gogol.

THERE WERE MOMENTS WHEN De la Estrella seemed on the verge of losing his voice; he'd gasp, slur his words in an almost inaudible murmur. At others, he'd raise the volume with vulgar disproportion. Certain passages seemed as though they were being projected in exasperatingly slow motion; then, without any transition that might prepare the audience, a frenzied urgency seemed to goad him to rid himself of his memories of Turkey as quickly as possible; the words overtook him, jostling each other to spill out hurry-scurry like a river that's burst its banks. The Millareses, at that point, were listening to him with very mixed feelings. Even for the twins it was evident that this madman couldn't be taken seriously. The dwindling audience began to exhibit certain movements of irritation, impatience, contempt, combined with the natural curiosity to know the end of the story that little by little was careening toward the grotesque. What, then, was the humiliation the Licenciado had suffered, whose revelation he was delaying to the point of annoyance? For varying reasons, the Millareses wished his downfall to be shattering; an exemplary punishment, even harsher than the one they faintly sensed. De la Estrella's thick, mutton-like head was still leaning on his right shoulder, his gaze fixed, almost always ireful, his posturing unnecessary and excessive. His intermittent handwaving alternated between trembling and frenzy. The same was true of his speech. He'd pass from shrillness to a reflective detachment that could almost be called academic; then the facial muscles would relax and his mouth would round, his lips forming a delicate circle from which would emerge, by contrast, words that evoked something more putrid than precious. He'd arrived at the beginning of the events of the second day, the last, as he'd anticipated, of his stay in Istanbul. He must therefore be very close to filling in the gaps in which he was so willingly amusing himself. The dénouement would have to justify the mottled series of charges he'd hurled sometime earlier against the Vives siblings and, especially, against Marietta Karapetiz, accusations that must have been of sufficient gravity as to force him to leave the country that same day.

That morning, he said he'd awakened late, mired in a kind of mental fog, the price for a brutally late night and the excessive ingestion of wines and liquors from the night before. A few gymnastic maneuvers sufficed for the discomfort to wane and transform imperceptibly into a feeling of happiness he'd never known before. He stayed in the shower for a while, which allowed his there and now to come into sharp focus. Yes, he'd crossed the threshold of the Sublime Gate, and he'd slept his first night in the legendary Istanbul, in a comfortable room of a famous hotel, where, also lodging, were his friend Rodrigo Vives and his sister, the none-too-friendly Ramona of the same surname, to whom at that hour he allowed himself to be magnanimous due to the resounding—and involuntary, he must admit—victories he'd achieved over her the night before. Scattered images of the extraordinary woman with whom he'd dined and conversed in the most delightful atmosphere began to appear, of the pleasant Alexander, whom she called, indistinctly, Sacha, my little boy, Sachenka, little man, my little white dove. He remembered, as if through a clear mist, the meeting's tentative beginning, the missteps, the initial coarseness, perhaps, with which he treated a widow whom fate had treated with unnecessary harshness. He immediately took responsibility for the unpromising nature of an awkward beginning that might have spoiled an unforgettable evening. There were many extenuating factors that mitigated any judgment one might be tempted to make. To begin with, they'd made a lady whose time was precious wait an hour and a half in a public place; who, what's more, had come with the expectation of meeting Rodrigo Vives, that nothing in the making, and hadn't the slightest goddamn idea she'd have to dine with a total stranger and his friend's unbearable sister. Those early inconveniences dimmed to the point of fading almost into memory. There glowed, instead, the radiant moments, the wonderful smile of a lady of the world; the brilliant, wise, and passionate language of the woman of letters; her peculiar sense of humor, at once refined and hermetic, before which a wide-eyed boy, which he surely considered himself at times, was forced to declare himself all but lost, or at least unsure, in her intricate labyrinth of verbal arabesques. He wondered what urge had prevented Marietta Karapetiz from declaring her nationality. If anyone really wanted to know, it would be the easiest of things to find out. She'd not even introduced Sacha by his surname since that might give a clue to the family origin. But, in the end, there's no woman who doesn't have her whims, her caprices, her private games, her intimate fantasies, and among civilized people it was an obligation of principle to learn to respect those closed boundaries of individuality.

"Meeting that personality," he declared, "was an extraordinary stroke of luck, something that didn't happen to everyone. I entertained myself by going over some of the qualities I'd noticed in her the night before. Profound knowledge of the history of Byzantium, elegance in her dress, authority in her gestures, a deep love for Mexico. I kept repeating all this to myself, trying naïvely to convince myself. A passion for my country so fervent that it seemed to border on delirium. I didn't want to take the blindfold off; I refused to recognize that all that was a mirage, a false Eden, a deceptive Fata Morgana, an Olympus made of materials of the most primitive sort. It wasn't going to take long to uncover the imposture! In the shower, I remembered the sheen of eccentricity that her conversation at times exuded; whimsical detours of language, expressions that no self-respecting lady would allow in her presence, rambling soliloquies, whirlwinds of incongruity and even brazenness. But what did that matter, compared to her virtues? On the other hand, a woman of letters could allow herself certain whims that someone like my sister or María Inmaculada de la Concepción, my beloved wife, would never even dream of. She insisted on deceiving me to such a degree that I became convinced that every time I detected any capriciousness, contradiction, or flagrant vulgarity in her language, it was due to the personal limitations of my comprehension. So dizzying was the speed of her mind that it was difficult for those who listened to her for the first time to understand the content of what she was saying: I caught the chaff, but the wheat escaped me. My humiliation knew no bounds. Despite the drubbing she gave me on more than one occasion, I wanted to remain scandalously submissive. A pitiful case of self-deprecation. I remembered that the night before I'd started off acting a little cocky in front of her, only to end up soon after wallowing at her feet, begging her to continue mistreating me: 'Flay me, little dove, rip me to shreds, flatten me with your hard, beautiful shoes, with your exquisite cut-crystal heels! Return me, madrecita, now worthless, to the miserable sludge I should never have crawled out from!' Not to be believed! Minutes later, while having breakfast in the hotel's almost-empty restaurant, I was able to remember more clearly her words of farewell: 'Brilliant young man, you have much to give to the world! You're not finished here; your look is telling me so . . . !' These words drove Ramona mad with envy, but, above all, those she spoke moments later, when I said goodbye to her for the second time, which no one but I and perhaps Sacha had heard: 'I sense in you, beautiful young man, exquisite virtues. You, my friend, are a man marked by light. Do not abandon yourself, I beg you. It would be a crime against yourself and against those of us who have glimpsed the existence of your potential prestige.' I felt an invigorating current run through my body as I repeated those little words to myself again. Now, tell me, was my giddiness not understandable? I was a wholesome, callow youth. No one had ever said such things to me. People tended to regard my intellect with contempt, to treat me like a profligate who was making his way in the world by questionable means and a bit of luck. Despite her congenital foulness, Marietta Karapetiz revealed me to myself. That's the only thing I truly give her credit and thank her for. That morning, at breakfast, I had my first awareness of being a new man. I saw my life, my past, present, and, above all, the future in a different light. I wouldn't abandon law; at least not entirely. But my mind would make room for new interests. I'd devote myself to activities that until the day before I'd considered only suitable for poofs and impostors. I remembered the words of the aging warrior who converted his enemy to the faith of Christ and repeated them to myself with the utmost solemnity, 'Haughty Sicamber, bow thy head; burn all that thou hast hitherto adored, and adore what thou hast burnt!' I too would study anthropology. I'd read with devotion the giants of ancient Russia. I'd learn as much as I could, and later I'd carry on with her, my teacher and benefactress, a long and passionate correspondence; I'd ask her for advice and direction in the event I needed them. I'd give her repeated assurances that I'd not abandoned the path, or, simply, I'd set out for her my views on the world, society, the arts. What a fool! That was me, the most monumental idiot history has ever produced. However, I swear to you, I don't regret having carried that cross. For better and for worse, that encounter was decisive for me. Not to follow in the steps of the Divine Heron, as I believed then, but to later deliver her to the pillory, to unmask her a thousand times, to strip her naked before readers, to expose the obscene scar that marked not only her belly but also her soul. I didn't wait to return to Mexico; while in Rome, I prepared to do battle. I was determined to know more than she did and to refute her thoroughly. But in order to do so, and these are the things that no one ever thinks about, I needed to obtain certain economic means. Only if I was free of that concern, which, I was certain, my studies wouldn't be able to provide, would I be able to devote my time to research. I began to work systematically in various directions. To my mind, a rich heiress is always the perfect solution to many of life's great problems. I don't know any man, say what they may, who'd turn his nose up at bagging a rich woman. What happens next is another story. First you determine the price, then you have to pay it. And I want to see you there, *cari amici!* It's not that marrying a poor girl is a joy. No, perhaps the solution lies in knowing how to choose the right rich women. The very idea of spending my whole life next to Ramona Vives made my skin crawl! And whose wouldn't? I didn't marry her, but I didn't gain much in the exchange either. One could almost say that it was the opposite. When I returned to Rome I wooed four or five girls from good families. In those days, scholarships weren't as easy to receive as they are today. Students who went to Rome were usually supported by their parents; that is, they had to be people of means. I was one of the few exceptions. I became the obligatory beau of every young woman who came along. Or rather, I tried for a while, without much success, I must confess. I got bored; I always ended up going back to the dry cleaner, and a fling now and then, of course, with waitresses, maids, salesclerks, real women, without pretensions, maternal, which is what men look for when they live away from their family. All the Mexican girls thought about was going out dancing every night, dining in expensive restaurants, going to expensive cinemas, having coffee and ice cream at Rosatti or Canova, which were very fashionable places then, or, even worse, going to bars on the Via Venetto, where just to breathe cost a fortune. So I decided to shake them off. A good plate of pasta, a dollar in the bank, and a place to sleep, even if the bed smelled, was worth more than all the whims of little rich Mexican girls with their immaculate underwear and perfumed armpits. That wasn't the way to go. The situation with María de la Concepción presented itself in a different way. One day my friend from the Consulate came to see me; he told me that some girls from Mexico had arrived and that they were trying to locate me. They were none other than the García Roviras, mother and daughter, from the upper crust of Piedras Negras, whom back home I only knew by sight. Someone had told them that I was living in Rome and that I might be of use to them. I have no idea what they could have imagined! Perhaps that I was working at the Embassy and earning millions of pesos. My friend invited me to have dinner with them, and so I began to associate with Concha and her mother, who turned out to be the daughter of Italians. They were to spend six months in Rome, they said; and then they'd make a brief tour of some other cities before returning to Mexico. They were staying at the home of the mother's family, because paying for a hotel, renting an apartment, wouldn't even cross their minds. I found no one in the family to be likable, neither the Italian relatives, nor María de la Concepción, nor her mother. But the food at the house was very good, and my fellow countrywomen were at times generous; it all depended on the mood you caught them in. They began to invite me to the cinema so that I'd translate the movies for them, then to go here and there, always with an ulterior motive, since they weren't able to get around without an interpreter. Before I knew it, I was going out with Concha alone, without her mother as chaperone. A girl at that age who's decided to pay no attention to her weight tends to have certain eccentricities. For example, we were to call her Concepción, or María de la Concepción, and never Concha, as she was known throughout Piedras Negras, because she'd been told that outside of Mexico that word was an affront to decency, as it's an epithet for the female pudenda. One might have thought that even if the most lascivious-minded male called her Concha, Conchita, Conchón that the mere sight of her would vanquish any feelings of lust, but that wasn't the case! Not in the least! Sometimes, when we'd pass by a bookstore in Piazza Colonna, I'd stop in front of its shop windows and sigh conspicuously. She'd sigh too and say: 'By the way, Dante, I'd very much appreciate your advice, since you know so many things. I have to buy a present for one of my cousins, he's about your age, and I really don't know what to give him. He likes books, at least that's my impression. What would you give him if you were in my position?' I'd mention a title and show her the cover over and over until it was etched in her memory, as she was slow to catch on, and the next day I had the book in my room wrapped as a gift. Of course, I made sure they were always quality editions. After all, she'd say she wanted the book to make a good impression. The second or third time, after asking the question 'What would you give him if you were in my position,' she was careful to specify 'that's not too expensive.' She was slow-witted, yes, but no one could beat her in guile. One day I conveniently stopped in front of a shoe store, and I repeated to her the little speech I'd heard so many times from my pal at the Consulate, and I concluded, just as he did: 'The impeccably dressed man needs to wear English shoes on certain occasions; but it's not enough that they're English, they must be of this or that brand depending on the time of day. A gentleman who prides himself on dressing prop- erly must have in his closet at least one pair of Church's shoes. I'm penning right now, as a matter of fact, a little essay on the influence of dress and footwear on the social life of nations. An exciting topic, you have no idea. What stinks is having to write it from memory. What else can I do?' And a couple of days later at the door of my building I was told that the usual hippopotamus—the Romans are that direct—had left a package for me. My heart was pounding. I was sure María de la Concepción wasn't going to fail me. When I saw the dimensions of the package, the illusion was deflated. I all but forced myself to open it reluctantly. It was a paperback book on the history of footwear. Please don't make that face at me. I'm not going to bore you with the history of my engagement, much less the tribulations of my married life. Those are very private matters—sacred, if you ask me. There are people, certainly most of those who have to deal with her, who think she's a repulsive woman, cheap to the point of avarice, a veritable shrew. I don't give a good goddamn if they think that I've become just another one of her employees, that I earn less than her chauffeur. Let them talk. I'm satisfied to have successfully overseen the development of her properties in Cuernavaca, along with the construction and sale of the houses, and to have helped increase her daughter's inheritance. I have my story and the world has its own. There are those who make fun of her bad disposition, her flesh, alas, of a massiveness that no longer borders on the grotesque, as before, but on the titanic! Let them! They'll gain nothing by it. When I met her she was, shall we say, a plump young woman; she wanted to outdo herself, to double, triple her size; there are those who like that, each to her own taste! If she didn't want to look like a whale that had just swallowed another whale, she'd have followed a diet, submitted herself to some regimen. Why worry about what she's indifferent to? I repeat, I've not brought up this subject to mock her, nor to complain about the minginess with which she treats me, but to emphasize the influence that the events of Istanbul had on my later life. Thanks to the generosity that Concepción showed at that time, I began to build a small library; I acquired, for example, the complete works of Gogol, a biography of him, and one or two books on Russian literature. I'd made it a condition of accepting her gifts that we both read the books. More than once I'd heard her say that reading was her greatest passion, that since she was a child, she'd read voraciously. I'd pass a book along to her, and she'd return it to me the next day, or at the latest two days. She'd swear over and over that she'd read it, and that everything in the book had seemed precious to her; yes, she'd loved reading it, she'd tell me, her eyes lowered and in a voice that sounded as if butter wouldn't melt in her mouth and she were kneeling before her confessor. I imagine she read the flaps, perhaps a page or two, because from time to time she got something right, but even in those cases she gave the impression that it was little more than dumb luck. Without realizing it, I started to become preoccupied with her education. I wanted to make her a participant in my introduction to literature. I talked to her about my favorite author; I recounted the plots of his novels, stories, and comedies. I shared with her what was written about him in the treatises on Russian literature. She'd walk beside me, silent and with her eyes lowered, and would raise them only when we passed by some food shop whose windows seemed to revive her. Poor thing, I thought, she's not had the benefit of a good education, but I'll see that she acquires one, which is even more important in a woman's life than in a man's. One of the books I lent her—and you can imagine how interested I was in her opinion!— was Gogol's collection of tales titled *Mirgorod*. One of them was of special importance to me, 'Old World Landowners,' which Marietta Karapetiz had analyzed during my meeting with her, and about which I wrote my first article, refuting her. The result was the same. She returned it to me the next day with the same inexpressiveness as always, repeating the very same thing, that yes, it was very nice, not to be believed, remarkably beautiful, with the massive, obtuse face of someone who's never dreamt of anything but legs of jamón serrano and roasted duck. I asked her if she really meant it or had just said it to agree, and, without moving an eyebrow, she answered that she'd liked it, of course, she'd liked it a lot, tons, and when I asked her what it was about, she said Russians from another time, from the old world as the title suggested, about their life, their religion, and all those things. That day I felt more than fed up; I wouldn't have cared what she said about any other book, but that one was different. I kept pressing her. About Russians, of course, that was obvious, since the author was a Russian, but what was it about? With stubborn obstinacy she kept repeating that it was about the customs of another time, that is to say, those of the old world, the religions they practiced, and other such blither. And when I insisted that she explain to me what those customs and religions were, she answered very curtly that it was time that I realize that as long as she could remember she'd always read, but that she didn't have a memory for repeating word for word; she read for enjoyment and enlightenment and not to recite everything verbatim, and that if I thought she was nothing more than a parrot I was very mistaken. She turned around and went home alone, and that night I had to pay for dinner out of my own pocket. The story of María de la Concepción and the old-world landowners didn't end there, but months later a sequel took place in Mexico City that defined the tone of our relations forever. By that time, certain events of transcendental importance had occurred, not for the destinies of mankind but for my own. I'd been married to María Inmaculada de la Concepción, which she'd taken to calling herself at that time, because María de la Concepción was no longer enough. I defended myself as best I could. I knew that I'd not been the only person to whom she'd given a book here and there. It became public knowledge that in the building where her aunt and uncle lived, and in the surrounding area, she maintained an extensive and frequent network of friends who had benefited from her largesse. Eugenia, one of her cousins and confidants, informed me that she'd given shirts and ties to a cab driver; bottles of brandy and expensive wine to a hairdresser; a Haste watch to a barista; shirts, shoes, a suede jacket, and a bathing suit to the waiter at the corner trattoria—which was rather middling, I might add—and, on more than one occasion, cold hard cash, which she also gave to the butcher's assistant across the street. To think that Little Miss So-and-So had skimped on buying me a pair of shoes! Her mother and the other relatives realized, of course, that not only did those roughnecks who lived with their hand out have nothing to offer a young girl in a compromising situation, apart from their bright eyes and long eyelashes, but that it was almost certain that, were they to hand over their portly little girl, who was so disposed to the delights of the flesh, to one of them, the happy husband would make her dance to whatever tune he played, and soon it would be they who walked around all dressed up, with a ruby tiepin, while she'd have to cover her vast frame with one pudgy hand in front and the other on her derriere. I offered them, on the other hand, a university degree and a more controllable personality, simply because I was Mexican and had aspirations of advancing in my career. They started by offering me the sun and the moon, and, of course, I let myself be duped in the most unscrupulous way. They made me travel to Mexico—so long, doctorate!—and they set sail on the next ship, hoping to salvage I don't know what appearances upon arriving in Veracruz, where the rest of their family would be waiting for them. Once they arrived in Mexico and held further discussions with relatives, two uncles and various brothers, and after I threatened to cancel the engagement because I believed they'd not kept the promises made in Rome, I ended up, almost out of boredom, signing all the papers that were put in front of me and going ahead with it. In the days that preceded the wedding march, I found her attitude had improved; she'd become more communicative and at the same time less confident, which in her case meant less obtuse. She spent her time tidying up the little house where we would live in Colonia Roma. Such humility, such a good disposition, led me to come to terms with the family. I no longer asked her as often about her reading, but rather I occupied myself by commenting on mine, providing a few small lessons, in small doses, to cultivate her brain as much as possible. Among other things, I pointed out the importance in the story of the landowners of the parodic games with which Afanasy Ivanovich and Pulkheria Ivanovna filled their leisure time, which lasted all day and all night. She nodded in agreement. I have no doubt that her mother and brothers kept her apprised of my objections, of what I'd told them about the relationships she'd maintained with butchers, chauffeurs, and waiters in Rome, paid for with money and expensive gifts, about a paternity that could be infinite, about my demands that there be no prenuptial agreement and that all assets be shared, the control of which should be entrusted to me. She seemed to take it all as a matter of course, as if those were the rules of the game, and I couldn't be expected to behave any other way. Whenever we arrived at a thorny issue, she'd change the subject and ask me to tell her about the games the two old Russians were playing in Gogol's story, and then I'd repeat, in the voice of a decrepit old man, Afanasy Ivanovich's arguments for going to war and becoming a national hero, just to rattle his poor wife, who'd start to play along with the joke and end up becoming truly frightened. María Inmaculada de la Concepción would celebrate me with applause and hearty guffaws for my performance as the old man, especially when I descanted on the need to divorce my old companion in order to look for a younger woman. In that chapter, if you'll allow me, the little old couple half in jest would reproach each other for the ailments that afflicted them in their old age and, from time to time, rehashed old wounds, only to end up shortly thereafter raving about their shared connubial love. Little by little, she began to play the role of Pulkheria Ivanovna, which in the end led me to make a fatal error. Aware that, out of shyness, and perhaps embarrassed by the speed with which her already voluminous belly was growing, she wasn't able to open her heart to me as it might have been necessary, I invented games similar to those in Gogol's story, n which we, no longer pretending to be the old-world landowners but not completely ourselves either, but only in the abstract, an immensely fat woman and a young intellectual with a brilliant future,, allowed ourselves to tell certain truths that propriety would not have allowed us to air otherwise, which helped us to lighten our unpleasant situation; that is, they served as an escape valve for the terrible stress we endured until our wedding day, a day memorable and fateful for everyone. Yes, during our playacting I reproached her with rather harsh words for the lust to which she'd surrendered herself upon meeting those boys in Rome, that incontinence of the senses that she hadn't even spared yours truly at a moment when I only wished to serve as her friend and refine her taste a bit. I pointed out to her the risks that a woman by nature so unprepossessing could run by falling into unscrupulous hands. And she, with her churlish sense of humor, answered that she'd never known hands more unscrupulous than mine in her life, but that the time would come when the ghastly heifer would transform into a graceful swan of magnificent beauty. I had to give her many passionate kisses to free her from the spell to which she'd been condemned by an evil and jealous witch from the very moment of her birth. We'd do our playacting, relax, then laugh at our own vulgarity, and then she'd invite me to dinner at the Bellinghausen, or, rather, to watch her dine, because I ate normally and spent the rest of the time contemplating her unrestrained gluttony. That was our life until the big day finally arrived. The wedding, yes, ladies and gentlemen! The festivity was held at the house of the bride's aunt and uncle. I don't know who did me the blasted favor of inviting my sister Blanca. Where they got her address, only the devil knows, because I didn't even know it myself at the time! Her unexpected presence, the rudeness with which she treated me in front of my in-laws and other guests, made me so tense that I'm certain if someone had put a piece of wood in my mouth I would have torn it to pieces with my teeth in a flash. Imagine for a moment the bride, whose appearance months of pregnancy had amplified in a prodigious way, hell-bent on wearing a white dress, a little tulle veil, and a crown of orange blossoms, and it will give you a visual image of the celebration! Everywhere I looked, I saw furtive and malicious glances, mocking gestures, giggles, what am I saying, guffaws, which no one bothered to conceal. My brothers-in-law were patting me on my shoulders, my back, making the most salacious jokes one can imagine about my relationship with their own sister. What's more, I'd been made aware of the plunder to which I'd been subjected: the only financial rights I'd ultimately been granted were those of administration, and even they were subject to so much supervision and control that rather than a manager I turned out to be little more than a mere employee of my wife, without salary. Because of all of this I let alcohol get the better of me that day. Not to mention the wretched quality of the booze. Within moments of getting married, I was already hammered. I began to perform, to engage in my usual monkey business in front of my bride, acting out scenes similar to the comic sketches that had delighted us so much during the previous days. I pulled my most theatrical voice from out of my chest, somewhere between booming and moaning, gave the floor a few taps, and planted myself in front of her, who at that moment was devouring a queen-size piece of wedding cake. Without fanfare, I said: 'No, no, and no, Doña María Inmaculada de la Concepción of the Open Drain! The time has come for me to tell you how fed up I am with the ridiculous spectacles you make me perform before the world. I assure you that at the first opportunity I'll divorce you. I'm only waiting for you—*o sole mio!*—to calve your Roman offspring, which I imagine will be any day now, and I will go find myself a svelte woman, a tiny spider, a twig, and not a colossal vulgarian like you.' It was a game, she knew it. Every day we acted out these kinds of scenes, with much stronger words, and we'd fall over laughing. But I didn't count on the psychological pressure that the environment can exert. Her relatives, the guests, everyone was frozen in astonishment, foolishly believing that I was serious. My mother-in-law rushed to embrace the chimera that her entrails had spawned. All that must have frightened her, and a person in fear, especially a woman, becomes unpredictable. María Inmaculada de la Concepción pushed her mother to the side and stormed toward me like a hurricane, lashed at me, hurled me to the ground, and kicked me with criminal fury. As I protected myself from her blows, I began to scream, 'Come to your senses, María Inmaculada! Think of the child you're carrying in your womb! Don't lose it!' She left me bleeding like a Christ, amid the applause and the hearty guffaws of those present, including, of course, my little sister, who was spurring her on to show me no mercy. The bride's wantonness defined forever the tone of our married life. Of course, every night I had to smother her with kisses and tickles to undo the evil witch's spell so she could become the sylph she was deep inside. 'This too,' I said to myself, 'was the fault of Marietta Karapetiz, who enticed me to read that story from which I received such harrowing suggestions.'"

"And you've been living apart from your wife ever since?"

"That's a matter, and you'll forgive my frankness, Doña Amelia, that I don't consider appropriate to discuss in public. It would be like taking advantage of my wife's absence to speak ill of her behind her back. To become entangled in the brambles of my marital tragedy would be to stray from the subject I've begun to sketch, that of the trip to Turkey, the humiliation of which I was the victim at the hands of the enemies of my soul, as well as some of its subsequent consequences. Let's put the wedding digression aside and return to the events that concern us. After breakfast that morning, I thought it appropriate to go say hello to Rodrigo Vives and inquire about his health. I phoned from the reception desk. His voice was still very strained, perhaps more so than the previous afternoon. He said he'd not slept badly, but that he'd awakened with a slight fever. That morning the doctor had dropped by and advised him to stay in bed for a couple of more days. Damn it to hell! What could I do? He asked me to come to his room to talk for a while. I went up immediately. Among other things, I needed to know how we'd settle the matter of money while he stayed in bed. How could I possibly consider myself a guest if he insisted on staying in his room the entire time? I wanted to avoid any future difficulties with his sister when it came time to pay any tabs, so it occurred to me that we should set a fixed amount per day, whether I spent it or not. It would free me from the embarrassment of having to depend on Ramona. Anyway, when I walked into his room I was horrified. One day of fever was enough to rob him of his flesh and give him a cadaver-like appearance that would frighten anyone. I was particularly struck by his eyes. They seemed out of place, markedly unalike, asymmetrical, so much so that later it was difficult to decide if they were too deep or, on the contrary, bulging. The only thing I remember is that there was something unusual about them. At one moment his face possessed an unusual brightness, only to change imperceptibly to total opaqueness. The same was true of his conversation. He had moments of excitement when he seemed to be animated by an electric current and spoke as if a faucet had been opened through which all the words that the human organism can store escaped, making his speech seem unintelligible. Then he'd suddenly begin to lose all his energy. He'd stop at every vowel, so that every word, not to mention every sentence, became unending, until his strength was completely drained away, until he was prostrate, but only for a few minutes, and then he'd begin again. I asked him about Ramona. Wouldn't it be a good idea to call her? He answered that she'd come to see him very early in the morning, that they'd had breakfast together. 'She's going to spend the morning doing some shopping. She wants to look at dresses, shoes, jewelry, those things chicks are interested in. Great! That way she won't bother me. Karapetiz's widow phoned me a moment ago. It's a shame I didn't go out with you last night!' And then I told him what a revelation it had been meeting that invigorating and incredibly learned woman. I gave him the best synopsis I could of her comments on the present and past of Istanbul, on Gogol and other Russian writers, and, of course, on her travels in Mexico. I added that we'd been joined at the end by Sacha, her brother. 'The masseur?' he asked. 'I don't know him personally. I've heard Marietta mention him a few times. He took part when he was young in certain rituals that I'm interested in studying.' 'Quite a character,' I said, and then added, 'According to what she told us, he accompanied her on one of her first trips to Mexico. An eminently distinguished man!' And from that moment on a dialogue of the deaf began. I didn't understand anything, and I attributed it to Rodrigo Vives's feverish state. 'I believe,' he said, 'that he's a wizard at what he does. He made quite a name for himself in Funchal, Cascais, Estoril, those tony spots where kings went into exile. It was the only way Aram Karapetiz could continue his studies. What a tough time! His wife and brother-in-law were living it up whipping the bodies of who knows how many sacred monsters while he, like a wise ant, spent day and night organizing the thousands of index cards necessary for his essays.' 'What wife do you mean? I don't understand who you're talking about.' 'Marietta Karapetiz! Who else are we talking about? She did everything—fashion model, masseuse, who knows what else. They say she was a real looker in her day. The war did a number on those people. But apparently they didn't lack imagination.' I felt, as I did many times during those couple of days, completely lost. I insisted again, 'I don't understand who you're talking about.' He ignored me. For a moment he seemed to have dozed off; then he continued: 'Yep, a remarkable woman. Can you imagine her? Spending the whole day massaging the balls of one bastard or another then going home at night to help her husband, in a poorly lit, humid-as-hell room, with inadequate dictionaries, no ink, translate obscure Chechen or Dagestani texts! She seems to be doing okay now, doesn't she? She enjoys her classes, lives without any real problems.' Today, as you know very well, it's possible to talk about any profession, even the most dangerous ones, rather flippantly, which wasn't the case twenty-five years ago when standards were still quite rigid. The profession of masseuse wasn't, as far as I know, included on the list of acceptable pursuits for a lady. It's difficult, you can't deny, to associate a university professor with a female who spends several hours a day in steam baths surrounded by a swarm of naked men. 'What made it occur to you that she was masseuse? Where did you get such a stupid idea?' I asked him in what I imagine was a trembling voice. All the compliments that woman had paid me the night before were suddenly in shreds. When spoken by a university professor they have a specific value; when delivered by a masseuse accustomed to gratifying her clientele in the most shameless way amid soap fumes and all manner of sweat, they not only lose their prestige, they turn out to be a cruel joke. 'She told me herself,' the expiring man answered. 'Why? Where's all this interest coming from?' 'No reason, but I imagine she was pulling your leg,' I insisted, trying to cling desperately to utopia. 'That woman has imagination to spare; I could see that last night.' 'Yeah, maybe,' he muttered, sluggishly, then closed his eyes. He seemed to grow bored at that stage of the conversation."

"And you never saw Marietta Karapetiz again?" asked Juan Ramón, exasperated by so many digressions and circumlocutions.

"I wish that were true! On the contrary, she's about to reappear, young friend. If B did not follow A, and C, B, man wouldn't yet have come out of the caves," said De la Estrella sententiously, once again forming a perfect circle with his lips. "I decided to allow Rodrigo to rest and went for a walk through the city. I'd not found the right moment to address the matter that interested me most, the nature of my guest status. The revelation of Marietta's and Alexander's physical activities prevented me from doing so. I was about to open the door to leave when I heard Vives's fading voice behind me: 'By the way, what happened last night at the restaurant, any incidents?' 'Dumbona stuff!' I said to myself. I approached the bed again and with the most casual tone in the world I explained what happened: 'Nothing serious, Rodrigo, nothing that one could call serious. We were scandalously late arriving at the restaurant. I don't know if your sister told you. Señora Karapetiz was a little disoriented by the delay, perhaps at first she even resented us, but luckily, everything was cleared up. It was an enjoyable evening; we ended on the best of terms.' I wanted to recite the phrases that Marietta Karapetiz spoke to me as she said goodbye, despite the depreciation they'd suffered when I learned of that ignoble episode in her past, which I never could have imagined. But I thought there'd be a more appropriate opportunity to do so. He replied that he was very tired, that he was going to get some sleep, although he added incoherently that he wanted to read the newspaper and that I should come and see him at three o'clock in the afternoon. I have the impression he didn't even hear my answer about the night before. I went up to my room to look for the tourist brochure I'd gotten at the front desk that morning. I could start with Hagia Sophia, and, if there was still time, see the two nearby mosques, grab a bite, paying for it, of course, with my own money, because that's how the invitation was turning out to be, and be back at the hotel by early afternoon. I did none of that. I stretched out on the bed and fell asleep. It took considerable effort to rouse myself. I went down to the restaurant again, ate some fruit, and drank a disgusting coffee. I took a walk around the block because I needed air. I couldn't concentrate on anything I saw. I began to feel restless, anxious, full of bad thoughts. For the first time, I was concerned about Ramona's animosity. What had motivated it? Why had she shown such hostility? The din of the street somehow intensified my feelings of loneliness. My individuality was trying to impose itself before that cacophony of noises and voices expressing themselves in other languages. I became more and more depressed. At half past three I entered Rodrigo's room with a tentative step and unsure mood. The two women were there. Each was sitting on one side of the bed. There was a large bouquet of roses on a small table and another of white carnations on the dresser. As soon as I entered, a tomb-like silence fell over the room, without anyone attempting to disguise it. I summoned my composure, shook hands, kissed both women on the cheek, and said something to Rodrigo about the improvement in his appearance, undoubtedly influenced by the flowers and their distinguished bearers. A white lie, as Rodrigo looked horrible. Karapetiz exerted a spell on the others, that's for sure. All my bitterness disappeared when I saw her; what's more, I didn't even remember what Rodrigo had confided in me about her past. I thanked her for her words of support the night before: 'Señora, you've ignited in me a desire to excel. I feel that my efforts have meaning. I will begin wherever you suggest. Do you want me to read Gogol? I shall! You've already converted me to your faith. Do you sense the budding disciple in me? Believe me, I can't wait until the books necessary to reach the light fall into my hands.' My enthusiasm, which was real, was on the verge of exploding when I heard a fiendish little laugh from Rodrigo, who tried to hide it under the guise of a coughing fit, and the putrid shriek of Ramona: 'The barbarians, France, the barbarians, dear Lutetia!' which she exclaimed with a pathos that was at once fustian and offensive. She then added: 'Marietta, what do you say we let Rodrigo sleep for a while; he's already taken his pill and needs rest.' 'You're absolutely right. This dark swallow, who in happier days had the joy of flying over the majestic Mexican mountain ranges, bids you farewell. What if, Ramona, I send the papers this afternoon?' And she answered herself, 'No, I'll send him something lighter and more entertaining in case during the evening he feels like reading for a while.' 'Ladies, I'm at your disposal,' I offered, not knowing what they were talking about. 'I'm very grateful, De la Estrella, but it won't be necessary.' Ramona had abandoned the informal address with me, which meant that our relationship had grown more distant. 'I'll accompany Professor Karapetiz to her house to pick up some books,' and she again thanked me curtly. The Gogol specialist added: 'The time has come for the males to rest and for us absurd little women to move along.' With her mouth Marietta Karapetiz signaled to me that I should not go with them, but her eyes belied her expression; an almost imperceptible wink, a gentle languor in her gaze, a faint trembling of her lips, betrayed an exhortation to follow them. I was overcome by the suspicion that the psychic pressure I sensed had no other aim than to take her in a cab and save her the cost of getting home. A suspicion I didn't even pretend to fight. I thought that if something had to be paid, Ramona would have to be the one to do it, and I insisted: 'By all means! Of course I'll go with you! I don't think it's appropriate for two such pretty ladies to be out on the street alone at this hour. The tourist brochure itself states that a woman must take precautions here that in any other city would be unnecessary.' I stood up. From the moment we left Rodrigo's room we began to behave in a way that was very strange. The two women, determined to go alone, and I, resolute in my position, without paying attention or even listening to them. And so we walked through the lobby, out the front entrance, and before we realized it we were on the street. A big blue car pulled up beside us. A uniformed chauffeur jumped out, ran around the car at breakneck speed, and opened the rear door through which Marietta got in. With equal speed, he ran to the other side to open the door on the left, through which, almost in hysterics, Ramona entered. I didn't require any help. I opened the front door myself and sat next to the driver. His name, I learned later, was Omar. Whether they liked it or not, there was nothing the women could do now except force me to get out, and I didn't think they dared, as the facts later proved. I felt I owed the owner of the car an apology for misjudging her. The fault lay in the unrefined environment in which I'd moved. I judged all women by the standard I would apply to my sister. To think that I'd suspected Doña Marietta of requesting my company just to save on cab fare! That woman was above all the pettiness that I insisted on attributing to her willy-nilly. I turned my head toward her, filled with respect. I opened my heart to her; I wanted, at any cost, to be her protégé. I swore that I already considered myself to be one, that I wanted to better myself, to discover, to know everything. 'As a child,' I told her, 'I was aware that a higher finger was pointing me toward a higher purpose. Unfortunately, señora, I've educated myself alone, in conditions that weren't at all conducive to the spirit; my mind has had to rub shoulders with people of unspeakable vulgarity. Last night, however, on returning to the hotel, I sensed that something new was beginning to germinate inside me, a need, a thirst, as it were, to start anew.' I was surprised that she received such sincere words with gay laughter, to which she added: 'Thank you, my attentive friend, for your magnificent roses.' As usual, that woman had the power to catch me off guard. Should I have sent her a bouquet of flowers that morning? Or was that the usual way she thanked someone for the compliments they paid her? One of many things I never learned! I sputtered I don't know what clumsy apology while the two women released what seemed like rather venomous giggles. I started to say something about the scenery of Istanbul and nothing acceptable came out; about life in cosmopolitan hotels, and here again I fell flat on my face; I commented that I'd read that morning in the press a medical article that had impressed me, but after my nap I couldn't, no matter how hard I tried, remember what it was about. As you can see, it wasn't my day. So I changed my tone, shed my mask, and implored with all the sincerity I could muster, with sincere desperation: 'Help me, Professor, to move forward! Teach me to enjoy the pleasures of the proselyte! Tell me, I implore you, what I should read, what method I should follow! Please explain it all to me! In me you will find a lump of clay to mold, or wax if that is best to fashion at your holy discretion!' 'The chichi, señora, the chichi, dear Lutetia!' was my compatriot's new contribution. 'I was thinking of Gogol,' said Marietta Karapetiz, with a distant air, as if speaking from a dream. 'I'm preparing my paper for the Verona Congress. Gogol's drama stemmed, among other reasons, from not knowing how to detect what forces were at work in his society. This sounds like sociology, I hope not. He knew that these forces existed; moreover, he thought he could control them at will. When he discovered that this wasn't possible, he was so astounded that he lost part of his faculties forever. What a poor, marvelous genius of a man! The classic celestial lightning rod! He communicated visions whose origin he didn't know and that, logically, he attributed to a personal manner with which the Divinity favored him. He expressed an authentic inner truth, which he wrote about with confidence, without concessions. He was faithful, perhaps even in his final delirium. He was faithful to his soul, but perhaps not always to his body, if such a dichotomy is possible. We know little of his needs in this area, except that in one way or another they were anomalous and rooted in a deeply pathological core. The mystifications he tried to substitute for life eventually defeated him. When it saw him weakened, the Church, through the cruel arm of the Inquisition, took care of the rest; it plunged him into darkness, from whose depths he could no longer free himself.' She raised her voice. With exemplary severity, as if speaking with the voice of the inquisitor to whom she'd referred, she offered this admonition, 'Let us, my dear friends, always be faithful to the

instinct of life, as defections on that area come at too high a price!'
My nerves began to get the best of me. I couldn't tell which way the
wind was blowing. So as not to make a mistake, I answered bliss-
fully: 'So it is, señora, and so should it be! A good deed is never
wasted! Such is the apothegm that has always governed my morals.'
'You remember it, especially, Dante Ciriaco; betrayal comes at a
very high price. I know of cases in which defection has been paid
with defecation . . .' For several minutes she laughed uncontrolla-
bly, which to me seemed unworthy of her position, infecting with
her elation the mimetic Ramona and even Omar, the chauffeur,
who couldn't understand her because he didn't speak Spanish.
Suddenly, as if that brief playful interlude had never existed, she
returned to her academic tone: 'Nikolai Vasilyevich Gogol paid
that price. They disposed of him with unusual cruelty. First they
filled him with terror. They made him believe that the devil was his
confessor, that it was he who guided his hand in writing. The one
and only true author of *The Government Inspector* and *Dead Souls*
was called Beelzebub, Lucifer, Asmodeus, Ciriaco, no, no, sorry,
what am I saying, Satan. All of them, one and the same nature. He
became delirious. Three times he burned the manuscript of the
second part of *Dead Souls*, the work whose completion he'd been
announcing for many years, which sought to redeem Russia, that
is, the World. It's possible that the last burning was a mere fiction.
By then Gogol had already lost his creative faculties, and in his few
moments of lucidity he was aware of this drama. He'd never succeed in fulfilling the destiny to which he always felt himself called.
He'd never be the Angel who would redeem the Nation. It was then
that Matvei sprang into action. It was inevitable that he fall into the
hands of that cruel mystic and submit to him. The poor writer had
confessed to him what he called "his sin." We don't know what it

was, but we do know that he intended to atone for it. His only hope of being absolved lay in extreme penitence. So far we're moving in a mere tissue of hypothesis and conjecture. Is there some secret documentation that one day will come to light? I've imagined three or four solutions to the enigma, but I'm not convinced that I'm right about any of them. That sin rose before him like a haunting specter. It closed every path to him and reduced him to an immense living guilt. The whole of him was a wound. A wound that prayed, a wound that implored forgiveness, a throbbing wound that imposed the most atrocious penances on himself. Matvei forbade him to eat, forbade him to read any book other than a prayer book, forbade him to sleep more than two hours a day. Nothing was enough to achieve forgiveness. By the time his friends realized what was happening, it was too late. They could touch his spine through his abdomen. His stomach had become dry and atrophied tissue. A team of doctors gathered around the bed where he lay, all but a corpse. They bled him, gave him ice-cold baths, and as he was dying placed leeches on his temples, on his neck, in his nostrils, on the corners of his mouth. Before dying, he glimpsed a fragment, without understanding it, of course, of what was happening to him. He was aware of the existence of those ghoulish parasites that struggled to consume the last drops of blood his body still held. He saw them move about, swelling on his corpse-like face. He felt the gluttony with which those voracious mouths burrowed into his skin. He didn't recognize the faces of those around him; he managed only to understand that Matvei had been right, that he'd not managed to wash away his sin; the arms of the devil, whom he'd feared so much since his distant peasant childhood and whom he'd mentioned in countless passages, had taken hold of his remains. What little there was of him belonged to Satan. He expired amid howls and animal-like convulsions. He wanted to remove the devil's tentacles from his face, but doctors and nurses prevented him from doing so, holding his arms forcefully. The horrific penances had been to no avail. He saw himself walking, guarded by the vociferous legions of the Evil One, toward the eternal fire.' At that point the voice of Marietta Karapetiz became calm, she lit a cigarette, inhaled deeply, expelled the smoke, and, devoid of any pathos, concluded, 'But nothing such as that will happen to us. We will always try to act sensibly. We shall earn our own respect. Ladies and gentlemen, allow me to announce that you are at your home!' She seemed to have timed the story of Gogol's agony and death to the car ride. Indeed, the car stopped in front of an altogether uninspiring modern building."

VII

Wherein the already reluctant friendship between Dante de la Estrella and Marietta Karapetiz is put to a severe test, which will allow the reader to decide whether the relationship has ended or contemplates the beginning of a more intense phase, capable of overcoming the distance that will now separate them.

AT THIS POINT IN THE story, the narrator was visibly exhausted. With the air of martyrdom, the winces of suffering, the violent and uncontrollable tics, the dazed and fearful look, he seemed to embody to his listeners the final misery of Gogol, as it appeared in Señora Karapetiz's speech, which he'd recounted minutes before. On two or three occasions he attempted to speak, without success. He opened his mouth, breathed anxiously, panting, closed it with a doleful air, opened it again, until he succeeded at last in taking flight, and he didn't interrupt his soliloquy until finishing the story. He began in a modest, not-at-all-confident voice, which puzzled his listeners, so different was that tone from the phase immediately before.

"I scarcely remember what I saw in Istanbul. You remember that there was hardly anything there, you might say; you remember it—of course!—because you saw nothing. Very little, okay, but that little amount was burned onto my retina with all its richness of detail, recorded and sealed in my brain. From the moment I arrived at the train station until the night of the following day, when I returned there, escaping, I didn't allow anything to fade. I stored faces and gestures, unnecessary perhaps, of waiters, store clerks, drivers, simple passersby. However, if I return to the episode that took place in Marietta Karapetiz's apartment, my memory loses its exactness, hesitates, becomes muddled, and eventually closes. I explain it myself as a desperate reaction of the spirit to protect itself from the horror. You'll understand everything in a moment. Perhaps it would have been better to suffer a sudden attack of amnesia. To lose consciousness completely for a couple of months. And then gradually to begin to remember each step, allowing, of course, the episode that caused me the trauma to remain buried in my subconscious."

"What trauma?"

It was possible that, at this point, De la Estrella didn't hear any voices other than his own.

"That desired lack of memory only partially occurred. There are images that are very obscure to me. For example, of the building in which Marietta and Sacha lived, I only remember its shabbiness. An ungainly façade beyond description. It's also true that in those days architecture scarcely interested me. I couldn't imagine that it would play such an essential role in my life, and that I'd spend so many hours, all of them bitter, in my wife's real estate development in Cuernavaca, the mainstay of her fortune; a terrible job, Millares, you know it better than anyone; you, one of the first victims of her whims, her plunder, her greed. At that time I was blind to architectural form. Sometimes I was wrong, I'm not afraid to hide it. I confused styles, I made a fool of myself, especially in Rome, where people pay so much attention to such details. I'd declare that I thought a building was an eyesore, and people would reply that it was a jewel of functionalism, things of that sort. I had a rich sensibility, there's no question, but it was atrophied. I moved in a stale world, and it was natural for me to repeat the platitudes I heard around me. When I try to remember that building on the outskirts of Istanbul, all that comes to mind is that it was milky white, which I attribute to my blindness at that time. Well, the question of styles aside, I can certainly distinguish clean from dirty, and that dingy, flaking façade was, no matter how you look at it, grossly unpleasant. Up to that point, until our arrival, everything is more or less clear to me; what's no longer clear, I don't know if you understand me, or if you're even following me, is the haziness of my memory when I try to describe the apartment I visited. I see a very large space with one or two balconies, everything very faded, very gray. It pains me to offer such scant details, because if anyone prides himself on the accuracy of his observations it is I. I have nothing to gain by describing what's in this house or enumerating details that, I'm sure, would surprise you, because your familiarity with it would prevent you from noticing them. It's always the same thing, my God, the same thing! The bothersome branches that prevent you from seeing the forest! Nothing to gain, I repeat, because many years ago I was in this very room several times, when you, Millares, only spent weekends here, and today's visit allows me to notice the changes made; two bulbs, for example, are blown out in the lamp in the hallway, unless you've loosened them to save electricity; a spider has woven a web in the upper right corner of the bookcase, for several months now, because the web has thickened to form an oily, blackish crust. This isn't a criticism; there's nothing more alien to my disposition, knowing how unreliable help is today. But you would be astonished, I can assure you, if we paid a visit to one of your neighbors. Who lives in the house on the right?"

"Some Germans, but they're not there often. I don't know if they lend the house to someone or rent it; there are always different people there," Amelia Millares answered.

"It doesn't matter. Imagine if we were to enter that house, where I've never set foot, and sat down to have coffee with the owners, or with their tenants. No more than half an hour; just enough time to close a business deal. I can assure you that anyone would be flabbergasted. I could describe even the most insignificant detail of the living room, the color scheme of the curtains, what kind of collar the dog is wearing, the number of crystal objects in the room, their size, the space they occupy, that sort of thing, without anyone knowing that I'm subjecting the room to such rigorous scrutiny. I could almost say that I've possessed this ability since birth, and to tell the truth, it's a virtue that's never served any purpose."

"If there's anyone who shouldn't find it at all funny, it's the lady of the house," Amelia commented testily, "knowing that she has a snoop in her home who has nothing better to do than find dirt."

"Ask me, then," continued the Licenciado, "about the house of the Divine Heron, and you'll be left with the same chill I experience every time I try to evoke her pestilent lair."

"Nothing? Can't you remember anything?"

"Well, señora, nothing, in my case, would be impossible," said De la Estrella with exalted petulance. "I remember a large space, two balconies overlooking a street, and on one wall, behind a table piled with books and papers, the image of a Mexican Holy Child. If only I could forget that! But, please, all I ask is that you allow me to follow an order. I'm not Marietta Karapetiz, who develops three plots at once only to tangle them all up. If I despised incoherence before, from that date on, I've had a mortal hatred of it. When the car stopped and I heard the person in question say that we were in front of her house, even before she tried to open my door, the freaking Ramoncita, who, with all due respect, was already busting my balls, blurted out: 'Don't bother, Ciriaco, I'm going to get some books and be right back.' Ciriaco? Yes, ladies and gentlemen! Just plain Ciriaco! That obnoxiously cutesy girl had decided to intensify the offensive, but I didn't allow her to provoke me. On the contrary, I was the better person. To this day I'm still amazed at the composure I was able to muster in those days of impetuous youth. I was determined to be gallant and civilized, and I succeeded: 'It's no bother, Dumbona, don't worry. On the contrary, it's a pleasure,' and I started to walk toward the door of the building. Then the hostess intervened: 'Perhaps the girl talk we intend to have will bore you. When we women start talking about our own affairs we can be insufferable, I assure you. Omar can take you wherever you like and stop by in two hours to pick up Ramona.' She said it with such curtness that I was taken aback. But there again was the machination that troubled me; I was met again with the same wink as before, the same tender languor in her look, the same silent exhortation: 'Generous soul, don't abandon me! Pity me, your faithful admirer! Whatever you do, don't leave me alone with this silly and petulant little girl!' So I started walking toward the gate, entered the building, and headed straight for the elevator. They followed me like two little lambs. We reached the floor. The door was opened by a Turkish woman who was neither fish nor fowl."

"What was she, then? A cat?"

"I mean, señor, that she wasn't wearing Arab dress, but neither could one say that her clothes were Western. At first sight a trivial character, as nondescript as the façade of the building in which they lived, or as the celebrated Chichikov; she was neither tall nor short, fat nor thin, young nor old. But it was enough to linger on her face for a moment to discern that she possessed something perfectly defined. I've never seen so much wickedness concentrated in a pair of eyes, not even in the feral grimace she pretended to pass off as a smile! The first to enter was, of course, the home's owner. She handed the maid some packages and stopped in the hallway to welcome us. I skillfully rushed ahead of Ramona, fearing that she might go in first and slam the door in my face. By then I believed her capable of anything. Marietta Karapetiz gave some orders in Turkish to the plain-looking servant who came out to greet us and whom I will call Zuleima, since it was impossible for me to preserve in my memory the coarse name she was given. Zuleima asked us for our raincoats; did I mention that it was drizzling that afternoon? Before hanging them on the coatrack, I had the impression that she was spitting on mine."

"You're hiding something from us, Licenciado. Why had those women plotted to keep you from staying there? There's a mystery that you've been hiding from us for a while now."

"But of course they wanted me to!" the Licenciado screeched. "The only thing they wished was for me to remain there. They'd organized the festivities to the smallest detail, a surprise party for me! They must have started the preparations the night before. That was the reason for the encouraging looks, and the little sighs, and those silent little kisses that the hostess sent me from afar. I felt something strange, which was difficult to define, but I didn't imagine that it was a ruse prepared to such perfection. The Italians named the genre the *commedia dell'arte*! Without realizing it, I was already playing a role." He paused. "Look, Millares, I'm getting fed up with so many interruptions! Are you going to let me tell my story once and for all?"

"The floor is yours," said the architect, smiling.

"Did the Turkish woman turn into a rabid cat at the party?"

The storyteller looked at both the architect and his son with supreme contempt. Just as he had during the last part of the story, every time he began to begin again, De la Estrella cooed with his voice, softened it, as if he were telling a story to a group of children to help them fall asleep. It was the same on this occasion; with the tenderest of tones he returned to the house of Marietta Karapetiz.

"By the time we realized it, we were already in the room, about which, I've already expressed my regret, I only remember three or four essential things: The décor didn't center around objects of folklore or small exotic utensils as often happens in anthropologists' homes. There was no excessive use of Turqueries, or arabesques of any kind. There were, rather, if you will allow me, a few pieces of furniture, not many, of dark wood, with woven wicker on the sides and large green velvet cushions, a bit worn but very comfortable. At the back of the room, there was a large table, also made of dark wood, in front of a wall on which hung old prints, perhaps some masks, one or two African objects, and some framed pieces of tattered fabrics with green and ochre borders. There, you see? I have to take back my words. I begin to speak, my brain goes to work, and elements begin appearing here and there that I didn't know I'd retained. Of course there were exotic pieces, but they were justified by their antiquity, which is something else. It's possible that I can't remember more because there wasn't more. Nor is it my intention to meditate on the enigmas that the furniture and decorative objects of an apartment may arouse. La Divina walked us around the living room, making erudite comments about her relics. With her voice, gestures, the movement of her whole body, one leg moving back then forth, full of uncertainty, while the other, springing forward, confident, charged with a sudden audacity, with conviction in her gait, accompanied by facial expressions that in tenths of a second changed from mystery to surprise, from surprise to revelation, from revelation to ecstasy, Marietta Karapetiz was creating a kind of magical suspension, which reached its climax when she placed us in front of a modest frame, just behind her worktable. It was a popular print, on old, yellowed paper. She took it down, placed it on the table, and turned on a lamp, which bathed it in light. 'Here it is!' she exclaimed passionately. 'Ready to serve all who require it! I present my little boy and patron! Blessed, dear Holy Child! Friendly, industrious hand! Who but you flushes my entrails? Thanks to your kindness, Santo Niño del Agro, every morning I relieve my mind and heart of a dutiful portion of solid, superfluous shit!' Accustomed to her eccentric verbal frolics, with the memory still fresh of her reactions in the restaurant, believing that I was approaching her line, I exclaimed with servile emulation an '¡*Olé, torero!*' as resounding as hers from the night before. I expected at least a smile in response. It didn't come. 'Look at it from here, lovely, in this light you'll be able to see better!' La Divina suggested to Ramona. Had some demon possessed me? Was I seeking, perchance, my own perdition? The 'Ciriaco' that my compatriot had hurled so gratuitously upon arriving at the building, which I received so calmly, had begun to boil my blood. Delayed effect, I know, but certain. I began to gesticulate before Ramona, I must confess, in the spirit of a carnival barker, and, imitating her puerile voice, I shouted: 'Step right up, buttercup, and have a look-see! You're gonna love it, I guarantee! Don't be afraid, take your time, Little Miss Sunshine, come and worship this Holy Child who comes from your native land. Just you wait and see, he'll remove the sarsaparilla from your assparilla with a silver spoon!' Was I hanging a rope around my neck? I'll leave it up to you to judge! I took the image and put it under Ramona's nose. It was, indeed, a little saint with indigenous features. A child with an angelic gaze, wearing a crown and carrying a flowered staff. An air of perfect devotion and innocence. He seemed incapable of killing a fly, unaware even of his own existence. He rested on a throne that vaguely resembled a chamber pot, with verses at his feet. Marietta Karapetiz, with the voice and tone of a comandante, ordered me to read the text; it was the same litany I happened upon years later in an absurd essay by Rodrigo Vives published in a magazine in Mexico:

> *Little turd, come out,*
> *.out of your spout!*

> *Give me, I pray, a miracle today,*
> Santo Niño del Agro!

> *Whether I shit hard or shit soft,*
> *in the light or in the dark,*
> *be my patron, I implore,*
> *little Saint whom I adore!*

> *Protect your faithful,*
> *Holy Incontinent Boy!*

"Nothing! Not a smile, nor the slightest gesture of approval! What did it mean? Were we headed back to the same old tricks? What in the devil were they attempting with their funereal severity?

The women sat down, and I sat behind them. Marietta Karapetiz spoke again in that language, which I assumed to be Turkish but could just as easily have been Kurdish, Farsi, or Azerbaijani. What did I know? Were we, perhaps, among normal people? A pudgy little servant answered his mistress with a nervous stutter, while repeatedly nodding his head in affirmation. She didn't allow him to continue. She began to scream like a banshee, like someone in the middle of a field or in a market. 'Sacha! Sacha! Come here this very moment! Did you hear me? Did you hear me? Do I have to tell you that we're having tea?' And then, in a sickly-sweet voice, almost in imploring whispers, she added: 'Sachenka! Don't be coy! You know your dawdling drives me mad with anxiety!' A door opened, and the exquisitely debonair man I'd met the night before, the one in the impeccable white linen suit, suddenly appeared. What a difference! What waters was I wading into, I began to wonder. The shouts from the table had already seemed the height of vulgarity. Next to us were two servants, a woman and a little boy. Couldn't either of them have told Sacha that the table was set? But this lack of urbanity was nothing; on the contrary, it was Versailles or Buckingham Palace compared with the spectacle that unfolded before us at that moment. Sacha, as I have already said, burst into the room, his hair wet and disheveled, a towel around his shoulders, his crippled leg covered with some kind of garment fashioned out of white padding, fastened at the groin and the ankle. A spine-chilling spectacle! Few things are more immodest than the naked body of an old man. And Sacha's, covered by a thick white fur, which gave him the appearance of a faun in springtime, surpassed all limits, his pudenda waving gaily to the world. When he saw us, he stopped running, using one of his heels as a brake. His childlike eyes looked at us with mischief and consternation, then gluttonously skimmed the table. His huge teeth grew into a radiant smile of joy. At that very moment I remembered Rodrigo's revelations. Masseurs! Sacha's smile widened into the implausible. He apologized and added that he would join us in a moment. I looked at Ramona and winked cordially. A way to settle old differences, an invitation to close ranks against anarchy. I was offering her a peace pipe. We would soon see what the results would be. Marietta laughed contentedly, her heart delighted by her little boy's antics."

"Were they nudists?" asked Juan Ramón, with renewed interest in the story.

"They were something much worse. They were scum! Sewer rats, pretending to be animals of a different stripe! They fancied themselves, I imagine, sable martens, silver foxes. Pure trash! Masseurs from head to toe! That's what they were. I feared that we'd have to wait a long time while Sacha dressed and the tea got cold and the delicacies that filled the table became covered in flies, but it didn't take him more than a couple of minutes to return to the living room. He'd straightened his hair more or less, probably with his hand, and wrapped himself in an old striped bathrobe that reached almost to his feet. He was still barefoot, of course. The formalities began. The lady of the house stood up and employed protocol in a way that was surprising: 'My brother and I are highly honored by the presence in our home of two Mexican friends, Ramona and Ciriaco. Ramona and Ciriaco, we welcome you to this modest repast!' I stood up like a bolt of lightning. 'Ciriacanus the Brainless, who resides at ninety-five Heehaw Street, apartment seven,' I shouted in a shrill, high-pitched voice, 'is honored to consider himself the servant of little Sacha and of his adorable and refined sister, but above all else of the holy and miraculous Niño del Agro. Yes, friends, Ciriacanus of the Incontinent Anus and Little Miss Pain in the Ass, the child who shits through her piles, thank you for this honor and kneel before this noble and fraternal table.' I looked at the impudent matron with a sardonic smile that suggested, 'Come back at me if you dare, you shrew!'"

The Millareses, including the twins, had stopped laughing. They watched with apprehension as the man contorted, contracted, gesticulated, became physically smaller. An increasingly repulsive spectacle.

"Another brandy, Doc?" Don Antonio interrupted him.

"I'd prefer another whiskey. Very weak, almost symbolic, and please stop calling me 'Doc.' I detest abbreviations." He took a long sip and went back to his story: "I left them aghast. They served us, with great uneasiness, a thousand little things, almost all of them sweet. I couldn't stand them, such that I lost my appetite. I told them to bring me a glass of anisette. They felt cornered, I could see that. Marietta Karapetiz began to broach, in a submissive, almost pleading voice, Mexican topics, regional foods, indigenous festivals and their specific dishes; she referred to the bean tamales wrapped in aromatic leaves that some call yerba santa and others call tlanepa leaves, which she'd tasted one Day of the Dead in a cemetery near Xochimilco. 'It was so hard to travel your country in those days! We did it in carts, by mule, on foot, from sunup to sundown, far and wide. *¡Viva México!*' I must admit that I've had some very bad advisers in life: my sister, alcohol, and spite. I hold the last two responsible for what happened to me that afternoon. The small initial victories made me arrogant. I lost my sense of reality. I didn't want them to get away from me, to change the subject whenever they wanted, to impose the tlanepa leaf as a topic of conversation, or any other topic I'd not chosen. We'd get to Mexico later, when we'd settled accounts, made peace, and established the conditions of our future friendship. Perhaps I was overstepping my bounds in matters of form; in substance, the truth is that my demands were minuscule, ridiculous. I was only asking that this woman allow me to be her friend, her admirer, her disciple, that she stop referring to me by grotesque names, that she stop speaking to me cordially one moment only to ignore or pillory me the next, and that, above all, she cease to maintain such a humiliating distance between the treatment she afforded Ramona Vives and that which she afforded me. That was it! If you really think about it, it wasn't much at all. Nothing! To make her understand something as simple as that, it was first necessary to force her to eat dirt; then the time for the sweetest armistice would come. And with that worldly and carefree air that always suited me so well, I asked Sacha: 'So how's life? How are the massages going at the moment?' 'Ah, massage!' he answered with his eternal childlike air: 'It's going so-so!' he smiled, shrugged his shoulders, and continued: 'I'm not at the right age to give them anymore. My hands aren't the same; they don't have the necessary strength. Needless to say, I still like the work. I consider it an art more than a technique. I adore it.' He smiled again, as if apologizing, and added: 'I'm still at it just for the love of the art.' 'What are you saying!' his sister interjected, 'the things you hear sometimes! Just listen to him complain! Sacha has been like an ox all his life. He still is, look at him. He's as sturdy as steel! Once upon a time, when we lived in Portugal, he was known as the Steel Grip. He could put a dislocated bone back in place with the touch of a single finger.' 'What interesting things one hears in this house!' I added sarcastically. 'There's no end to what one can learn at your side.' I was talking like a sleepwalker, not knowing where I was going. Deep down it took only a few seconds for my morale to completely collapse. I'd imagined they were hiding their stint as masseurs as some sort of ignominious secret, a clandestine, shameful episode, the very mention of which would bring about their ruin, and the truth was that they flaunted it as a decoration of the highest order. 'Were your sister's fingers that strong too?' I asked, now without conviction. I was certain that she wasn't ashamed of that part of her past either. 'Of course they were!' Sacha answered me, bursting with fraternal pride. 'You have no idea how strong Marietta's fingers were; perhaps too strong. They were very powerful fingers, but they never lost their delicateness; her fingertips were full of imagination.' 'My clients called me Little Hands of Satin,' the interrogee shouted blithely. 'We were a sensational pair: Little Hands of Satin and Steel Grip.' 'Sometimes we swapped roles,' Sacha said, wresting the floor, 'according, of course, to the client's wishes. She'd become little steel grip, and my hands would turn into satin. People died of bliss. And don't think we were dealing with amateurs who could be satisfied with a pat or two on the back. No, señor, our clients came from the highest echelons, the nobility, Europe's great fortunes, the silver screen. In the morning we'd see their photographs in the newspaper along with the news of their arrival in Portugal and by noon, or that afternoon at the latest, we had them in our hands. We had endless fun.' The Divine Heron, her gaze lost in infinity, added, not without a certain ring of banality: 'A little frivolousness in life, however brief, is always welcome. For us, that was a veritable Golden Age.' 'They sought us out, begged us, offered us whatever we wanted,' her brother continued, brimming with enthusiasm, 'and there we swapped roles too. We were the real king and queen, and they were our submissive servants.' 'Two or three times a year a prince of royal blood would drop in on Estoril,' Marietta Karapetiz lowered her voice such that the name of the heir to the throne was inaudible. 'He'd show up with three or four friends, always the same ones, inseparable, it seemed, from school days. Strapping young men, very elegant, always gay, golden from the sun, men of stature, born sportsmen. For a few days everything was shouting, practical jokes, laughter, fados, foxtrots, and balalaikas. I'd go back home exhausted, but beaming with joy. Karapetiz, who was an extremely perceptive man, as soon as he saw me would say: "Don't tell me, don't tell me, I can already guess: the four frisky musketeers have returned to the baths." It seems that I was singing even in my dreams in those days. I'm afraid that by now none of those spirited lads are still alive. They had a lot of imagination, a lot of grace, and an energy that came from I have no idea where, as they carried more diseases than you'd find in a rat's coat. My God! You had to disinfect your hands with formol after giving them a good polish!' I wanted to die. I could hardly believe what I was hearing. Was this the same woman who'd spoken about my virtues and the bright path that lay before me? I imagined she'd restrain her haughtiness, clip the wings of her arrogance, and there she was speaking fondly of that ignoble profession. Ramona immediately joined in the cruel farce: 'How wonderful, Marietta! What a marvel! What an intense, playful current runs through every moment of your life! I envy you! I swear I envy you!' 'Would you also like to be a masseuse in a steam bath, Rabona?' I blurted out, but she didn't even answer me. I was just waiting for her to take her little notebook from her purse and jot down: 'Within a few years Little Hands of Satin and Steel Grip finished off the golden youth of several European countries.' At that, the hostess's gaze fell on our little Señorita Vives's stockings, and the two began to compare the design, the stripes, the material, at last bringing a bit of calm to the table. Sacha pulled his chair closer to mine, lowered his voice, and asked me to join him on the balcony to look at the view of the sea. The sea was nowhere in sight, but it was there that he begged me to be patient with his sister, to stop tormenting her, to bear in mind all she'd suffered, and he shared with me that she could have been a great belly dancer had hers not been disfigured by a scar that resembled a mouth that did everything but say mamá and papá. I couldn't breathe. I became nervous. I went back to my seat, determined to return to topics about Mexico, to tamales wrapped in tlanepa leaves if necessary. I raised my voice, interrupted the love affair between the women and their stockings, and said, determined to bring us out of the conversation on vapors in which we'd become lost: 'Your travels must have constituted a veritable Odyssey. I admire the courage and boldness of which they were proof.' Little Hands of Satin abandoned the conversation about stockings and threw me a curt 'What on earth are you talking about, Casianus?' I didn't bat an eye at the sobriquet, despite the rude way she'd pronounced it as 'Casi-anus.' Like an angel, I replied: 'Venturing out on the roads of Mexico during the revolution, señora, must have meant great risks.' 'The three of us were daring, tireless, three intrepid youths thirsty for adventure, if one could call my alte kaker husband a youth. People didn't call him *Kakerpetiz* for nothing. In reality, there were four of us. Traveling with us was a delightful man, whom everyone, including his wife and children, affectionately called Tagalong. He wasn't our guide, but a friend. He was from the Highlands of Jalisco, and in his lost moments he'd try to woo me. The four of us ate at the same table; we never treated each other differently. Tagalong had already attended the carnival of the Santo Niño del Agro twice and participated in the feast. It was through him that Karapetiz learned about those original ceremonies, and he offered to guide us. Indefatigable and daring, as I've already said, that's what we were. Sacha the most: he was the one who provided the example.

Nothing frightened him, not jungles, or deserts, or mountains.' 'No more than saunas, gymnasiums, or private baths,' interrupted the brother, whose spirit was still lost in the excitement of the steam rooms, 'which,' he added, 'I don't know if you are aware, can be more dangerous than the jungle. I remember an eccentric Sicilian, *il conte di Z*... It's a long story, and somewhat convoluted, but I can tell it to you in three words,' and once again he launched, along with his sister, into the lost circuit of Funchal-Estoril-Cascais, dwelling on trivial details of their work sessions, descriptions of twisted necks straightened by force, strapping biceps and flaccid glutes that a pat here and a slap there rendered as good as new, before arriving at the Italian count, whose blood pressure on more than one occasion dropped so low they were afraid they'd end up with a stiff on their hands. It was so difficult to steer the conversation away from massage that I resigned myself to coexist with the subject until it was time to say goodbye. But a stroke of intuition led me to ask them if they considered the mundane atmosphere of massage more attractive than the sacred ceremony of the Santo Niño del Agro. The sister and brother reacted to my question with a certain reluctance, due, I imagine, to how surprising the comparison was to them; then a profuse flowering of smiles appeared on their impressive mouths, exposing teeth so jagged that they incited fear. They began to eat with frenzy, with a Pantagruelian appetite. Honey dripped from their hands, the corners of their mouths, their noses, their chins. 'Well,' said Marietta Karapetiz at last, with a rather doubtful tone, 'the truth is that the two atmospheres would seem at first glance to be quite different, as if they required from the practitioner qualities of spirit that are on the surface incompatible; but, if examined carefully, the secret link that unites them is revealed. A feast in the tropics inevitably evokes fruits, flower necklaces, cinnamon-colored skin, certain music, the permanent awakening of the senses, the notion of the world as a mouth-watering delicacy. In massage, the body is also everything; the muscles play the role of fruits, the steam that envelops them is the humidity of the tropics. Allow me to tell you a few things; whatever conclusions you draw are your own. The feast to which you refer was famous for its richness of signs and mediations. I wonder if something similar could happen today. Of course, it would have other characteristics. We live in another time. If it were celebrated today, it would necessarily lose its solar character. It would be a clandestine ritual, which would detract from its fullness. And if it were public—I don't even want to imagine it!—its vulgarity would be overwhelming. Then, it was a pagan cult, an orgy, if you will allow me this charged word, whose purpose was to celebrate fertility. In that ceremony, men gathered life from Nature and gave life to Nature.' 'Because, you tell me,' Sacha chimed in with his usual exuberance, 'can there be anything more beautiful than moving the bowels under a blue sky, among floral scents, contemplating exquisite fruits? Don't you think it's nobler that the body relieve itself there than among columns of faux marble? Or, if you allow me to speak more plainly, how can it not be better for the soul to shit next to a river of crystalline waters, among herons of white plumage and clouds of blue and yellow butterflies, than doing it in a dark and putrid cellar?' 'If I may offer my opinion, to tell the truth, I prefer to do it in a closed place with proper sanitary facilities, and I don't care if the room is made of marble or adobe,' I responded with a certain curtness. 'The dilemma isn't so simple,' interjected the ineffable Ramona, blushing like a nun and in the most childlike voice in the world, 'because something in us succumbs to the lavishness of marble and something just as powerful repudiates that contrived pageantry and yearns for a closer encounter with Nature.' 'It's the triumph of the great pagan streak that fortunately still courses through our veins,' Marietta Karapetiz declared in sacerdotal fashion. Sacha's eyes sparkled with puerile innocence. In a parsimonious voice he recited with great satisfaction, 'Man is a thinking reed, yes, but we mustn't forget that he's also a reed that shits.' Each interjection followed the other in rapid secession. I couldn't take all that bombastic foppery any longer. I felt an excremental wave about to crash over me. I made a superhuman effort to overcome my repulsion and, with a trembling voice I tried to disguise as a coughing fit, I steered the conversation back to its ethnographic tourism aspect. I referred to the journey they'd taken through the southeast under the guidance of the famous Tagalong. I feigned interest in the characteristics of the region, its flora, its fauna, its orography. What were the principal crops? I asked them to explain why neither lentils nor chickpeas were grown in those lands. Had they ever tried to cultivate hops and malt? Were the settlers indigenous or mestizo? And what was the land ownership system? What was the nature of the celebration they'd attended? Was it of a secular or essentially religious character? 'We came at last to an immense clearing in the jungle, beside a river of wonder,' said the Divine Heron with a tone of resignation, as if she were a missionary. 'A place of marvels! When I recall the natural pageantry, I can say I've been allowed to know Paradise, but I also suffered in the flesh the drama of expulsion,' she stretched out a hand, clutched Sacha's arm with a gesture of pathos, and asked him, 'What sin could we have committed, little dove, to deserve such a severe punishment? My God!' she moaned, 'Is it possible that we'll never return to that valley of milk and honey?' 'We stretched out one hand,' Sacha was heard to say in a shuddering voice, 'and picked an unknown and marvelous fruit: a chicozapote, a mamey, a mango, a guanabana of prodigious size; we stretched out the other and touched the ass of a monkey of never-before-seen appearance and fur. Let's leave here, madrecita! Why are we waiting to return to those lands where everything is love?'"

"It stopped raining at last!" exclaimed Don Antonio Millares, getting up to open a window. Perhaps the Licenciado's visible distress and the gradual congestion of his face had made him anxious. De la Estrella had undone the knot of his tie and opened his collar. That simple detail added a rather unsettling charge of animalism and disarray to his appearance. "Yes," the old man repeated, "it's stopped raining. The fields needed water."

Salvador Millares also looked out of the window. He turned to the Licenciado and said:

"Your car has arrived. It's waiting for you."

"The sister and brother," continued the guest, without wanting to let go of the Istanbul apartment, "began by describing the place to me: an immense opening on the banks of a river interrupted by small islands of lush vegetation. Mangoes, tamarinds, palms of different species, yucca plants, which there they call izote, lianas, monkeys, herons, macaws, tapirs, giant ferns, as big as the mammoth that one day must have fed on its shoots. 'We'd returned to the primordial world,' our bucolic hostess declared. 'In the center of the opening stood three knolls, clear of weeds, painted a brownish color, with stairs dug into one side to facilitate reaching the top. They were hills, tall and spectacular, like chocolate cones rising in the middle of the green of the jungle. According to Karapetiz they could have been pre-Hispanic pyramids covered over by the ancient inhabitants to protect their mysteries. Time had done the rest. And at the top of each of them stood an adolescent. One wore the dress, crown, and flowered staff of the Holy Child, the other two were wrapped in some kind of Greek tunic.' 'Also the color of chocolate?' inquired Ramona, who'd begun to take notes. 'No, my dear, that would have been lovely, but the tunics were yellow, which, as you can imagine, suited them rather well. Each of the youths carried a small drum over his shoulder; they played all day long, at times in a slow rhythm, other times with a frantic roll. And that's how the morning passed. The first adolescent, the one who represented the Holy Child, was the young man who'd won the prize at the previous year's celebration. It wasn't so much the quantity that was being evaluated there as the form, which, as you well know, is so fundamental to any work of art. We'd arrived very early, at dawn, Karapetiz, Sacha, myself, and the likable Tagalong, our Mexican friend who'd revealed that world to us. An hour later, a crowd of celebrants of all ages were whirling around us, the women dressed in long white tunics and the men in long britches made of coarse white cotton cloth. On one side of the river there were toilets for the prominent women. The wife of the Cacique, the father protector of the region, owner of the river, Lord of the light, accompanied by his colorful entourage, would spend a good part of the day under a palm roof that was held up by log walls lined with splendid fabrics. We were allowed to witness the arrival of that elegant gynoecium in a boat that was itself a dream. A large white platform with mustard-colored sails with bright streaks of burgundy red. The landing was ever so elegant. The prominent women wore Greek tunics, their heads adorned with garlands of artificial flowers, and in their hands were beautiful little baskets full of apples, bunches of grapes, cherries, and peaches of colored wax. The Caciquesa was pulling behind her a tiny lamb whose wool had been dyed pink, its neck tied with a golden cord. An elderly woman who never left her side, perhaps her mother, an aunt, or a trusted servant, cradled in her arms an iguana with its mouth sewn shut, also with golden thread. Everything about them unrelentingly evoked Watteau's world. The tropics, it is well known, refine and soften everything, rendering everything exquisite, the learned Karapetiz often maintained. Once the woman in command was cloistered in her retreat, the ceremony quickly began.' 'They burned copal, myrrh, vanilla, incense, cinnamon,' added Sacha excitedly. 'They scattered rose petals everywhere. The earth's most beautiful perfumes began to spread across our field.' At that point in the story, we'd already finished eating. From time to time one of the siblings would reach forward to take a pistachio ball soaked in honey or a small chestnut pastry with sweetened coconut. After swallowing each morsel, she'd dip her hands in a small pot of hot water and offer her fingertips to Zuleima or the page with the swollen belly to dry them with dainty towels. Sacha didn't make use of those refined services; more often than not he'd rub his hands on his robe. The servants changed the cups, took away the teapot, and served us coffee. Strange, I know, but that's how things were there. After serving us, they sat a short distance from the table to enjoy the spectacle their masters performed. It was obvious that they didn't understand a word of Spanish, and yet they smiled without stopping. When the interlocutors paused, they nodded their heads in acquiescence. It would be impossible to find a better trained audience! The sister and brother seemed to have returned to the world of their childhood, so intense and spontaneous was their elation. Their eyes, their skin, above all, their gigantic teeth were sparkling. 'On a signal, the young men perched atop the knolls began to beat their drums in a frenzied fashion,' said Sacha. 'To which there was an immediate response,' his sister continued. 'Three, four dozen elders who were scattered and mixed among the crowd responded with a long blast of trumpets. The world was set in motion. People began to seek their place among the throng. The faithful took their places around each of the knolls, forming rings, like concentric circles. A sea of white, dotted only by the blackness of their hair and the flowers that adorned it, surrounded the three hills. The din began to subside. The rolling of the drums became quieter, delicate, almost sedate. The groups gradually fell silent. And suddenly, just as the man was in a kind of intense silent dialogue with himself, the bedlam started again: the furious roar of the drums, the fervid response of the trumpets, and the peal of a bell that hung from the branches of a mango tree that tolled with such dramatic effect that it seemed to announce the end of the world. Make ready your soul, o sinner! Cleanse your body, o sinner! Cast off what no longer serves you, o sinner! The first lady's compartment opened, more luxurious, I believe, than anything the Queen of Sheba might have known. She came out, followed by her ladies in waiting, and, raising her hands, displayed a vessel of precious silver, which she carried, slowly ascending the long steps, to the top of the great pyramid. With a courtesy as natural as it was refined, the sure fruit of an ancient culture, the powerful lady went to the young indigenous boy who was playing the little saint and helped him sit on the silver chamber pot she had brought. With a slow and cadenced voice, vocalizing each syllable with care, they both recited the prayer:

> *Little turd, come out,*
> *out of your spout!*

> *Give me, I pray, a miracle today,*
> *Santo Niño del Agro!*

Whether I shit hard or shit soft,
in the light or in the dark,
be my patron, I implore,
little Saint whom I adore!

Protect your faithful,
Holy Incontinent Boy!

"'That throng of mourners, positioned on an infinite assortment of vessels—chamber pots, lard cans, oil cans, braziers, soup pots, buckets, washbasins, plates, shoeboxes, or even modest pieces of banana leaf—recited the inspired prayer with devotion, faith, hope. A moment later the woman descended and made her way toward her quarters. It was said that she had at her disposal a box of perfumed cedar, with a hole that allowed her to lay eggs directly into the river. If the Child favored her, her fruits would feed fish and lizards. As soon as the doors of the privy of power closed, the true communion between Man and Nature began, the ecological feast, the dialogue between the human shell and its contents. For several hours the imploration was repeated over and over again, hypnotic and monotonous. The supplicants moved their shoulders rhythmically, striking their thighs with their fists to the beat of the prayer and stomping the grateful earth with the soles of their feet. Waves of delicate sighs, bestial moans, and trembling blandishments rose up. Imagine now the thousands of forces, and you'll have the most perfect, the most lamentable, and at the same time the most hopeful polyphonic poem.' Suddenly something, I don't know what, perhaps a distant car horn, awakened me from the lethargy with which the abundance of oily desserts, sweet liqueurs, magnetic chants had held me captive. What was happening! Into what

185

hideous coven had I been initiated by Little Hands of Satin, whose malevolent feat had gone all but unnoticed? All of us present, including Zuleima and the young potbellied man, were rhythmically striking our thighs, stomping the floor to the chant being intoned by that diabolical woman. One knows how one gets into these phenomena of subjugation, but never how one will get out. I stood up as if propelled by a spring. I told the hosts that I'd had a most interesting time; I think I even used the adjective 'fascinating' so that they would not suspect my dissatisfaction. I added, so as to make my departure seem natural, that Rodrigo and I had agreed to see each other that afternoon. 'I don't know, Ramona, whether you'd like to stay or to go attend to our patient,' I said, more than anything else to secure a return car. I took a few steps in the direction of the door. I walked over to the coatrack to pick up my raincoat. I mustered my courage when I saw that it was just a step away from the door and asked if it wouldn't be too much to ask, because of my unfamiliarity with the city and the possible difficulty of getting a cab, that Omar take me to the hotel. No one answered me. Ramona began to laugh like a madwoman. Perhaps that was what prompted me to shout that I wasn't used to listening to conversations like theirs, much less during meals. I'd grown up in poverty, but there, before that distinguished drift of pigs, I was discovering for the first time that my education had been superb. I wanted to add that only a miracle had prevented me from vomiting when I heard those stories, but I restrained myself; it was a good thing, because at that moment I felt Sacha's hand 'helping me' take my arm out of the raincoat. How he managed to get from his seat to the door is beyond me. His seemingly warm and obliging manner almost brought tears to my eyes. With the look of a playful dog that doesn't understand why he's being punished, he exclaimed, 'Don't leave so fast, my friend! Tell me, what's upset you? Why don't you like us?' 'These stories shock you, don't they?' asked, in turn, his sister with a sweet voice, a reflection of her total insincerity. 'You must look at them with pure eyes, the eyes of a child. They're carrying on the most ancient rites related to the consecration of spring. These are ceremonies that, as strange as it may seem, celebrate fertility, fullness, the plowing of the land, and the harvesting of fruits. The magic, in these cases, the folkloric charm and innocence, are only a veil. Their deepest poetry is rooted in praxis.' By this time the pressure that Steel Grip was exerting on my arm had driven me back to my chair. His sister, concerned, possibly by my reaction, gave one of the outrageous reversals I'd known her to give during our brief interaction: 'However useful these practices may be, I think you're absolutely right. There's something there that assaults our aesthetic sense, the deepest foundations of our morals. The disgust I felt on that occasion! Yuck! Just remembering it makes me nauseous! I admit that those ceremonies may have a certain rough charm, a certain odor of stables, of manure, which could be stimulating for people who like strong pleasures. *Nostalgie de la boue*, the French call it. But we are not all birds of the same feather. There are rooks and magpies, but there are also nightingales. The afternoon of that day became a magnificent torrent of filth: stench, shit everywhere, flies the size of eggs. Would you have me believe that some of those present, those from the enlightened sector, shall we say, sensed that mystical connection of the soul with the earth that demagogues proclaim so loudly, of the link between the act of emptying the body and the union with the divine, of which no less than the serene Ulpian spoke? Tell that one to someone else! I saw nothing but a fanatical and bewildered mass, drunk from the sun and bad odors, placed in grotesque positions, victims of unbearable stomach cramps, while the monkeys, also disgusted, passed by them frolicking, holding their noses, screeching like demons, trying to exorcise—the poor things!—the pitiful spectacle of that debased humanity. We were in the midst of the most disgusting coven imaginable. Yes, Cassiodorus, what was being celebrated there was the pure feast of the lower belly. At a certain moment, with another absurd roar of drums, trumpets, and chirimia, the Cacique's wife came out of her ostentatious quarters, which initiated—hélas!—the final ceremony. Some had received the merciful assistance of the little saint, others remained with their loads inside. I can tell you no more. The return of the germinal element to the barren dust had come to an end. What followed might not in itself be wrong, but the manner in which it was carried out was a vile mockery of all participants. We were up against the Court, its train of abjection, bribery, and complicity. It was necessary to choose the winner, to let him know that he would have to prepare himself for a year, because at the following feast it would be he who would incarnate the Holy Child. A truly solemn responsibility. I'm tired of talking..., sigh, the world suddenly became, I've already said it, don't let me repeat myself, something offensive and repellent, where everyone participated, the elite and the plebs. Sacha—that tremendous idiot!—had the prize stolen from under his nose.' 'Under my own ass, you mean,' the aforesaid corrected her, contrite. I've already said that I'd been wanting to leave for a long time. I felt nauseous. The heat was unbearable. The servants had replenished the table. The sister and brother went back to helping themselves to new treats and dripping honey. Not only was Sacha now wiping his hands on his robe; Marietta was doing the same. She'd dip her fingers into the little basin of water and wipe them on her brother's robe. I took a piece of cake; a whiff of sewage inundated my palate. I wanted to get up, look for the bathroom, expel my stomach contents, but again Sacha used his claw's hulking strength to force me to remain seated. An unnatural excitement reigned. Omar, the respectable-looking chauffeur, had joined in the revelry, and he too filled his fingers with honey and wiped them wherever he could, on a handkerchief, on Marietta Karapetiz's legs, on my pants. Masters and servants began to wink at each other, to laugh, first in an oblique, furtive way, then to burst out laughing, to speak in their mysterious language, to make horrible faces at me. There was an unimaginable moment when Ramona Vives, without anyone foreseeing it, left her seat, squatted down, and began to turn in circles, coming closer and closer to me. She wiggled her body, above all her hips, and moved her head from side to side in a comical, though unsuccessful, imitation of a duck's waddle. 'Quack, quack, quack! I'm looking for you, Quasimodo! Quack, quack, quack, quack, quack!' They all applauded and began to squawk just like her; the young servant with the huge belly and the once respectable Omar made noises with much less innocent lips. They surrounded me. To humor them, I joined in, 'Quack, quack, quack, quack! Quasimodo, quack, quack, quack, quack!'"

"And why in heaven's name did they call you such bizarre names, Licenciado?"

"I don't know. I never knew. That day I was Ciriaco, Cirilo, Casianus, Cassiodorus, Quasimodo! Why? Out of sheer desire to taunt me, I imagine, to humiliate me. How could it be that, in order to rid myself of the mockery to which they were subjecting me, I was the one who was forced to suggest—yes, I—as incredible as it may seem, that we return to the subject that so repulsed me! With what was left of my composure I managed to say: 'Friends, I urge you not to interrupt further the story of our illustrious hostess. Let us give her time to finish the learned ethnographic exposition she's begun. Tell us, dear Professor, what happened next!' 'As it happens, many things happened,' she answered, now a bit more serene. 'The jury met to deliberate the awarding of the prizes. I don't remember what criteria were followed; nor does it matter, because it was all a fraud, I'd need to reread Karapetiz's account,' she answered me, and suddenly with a gesture and voice of concentrated venom, she added: 'But you're relentless! *¡Sí, señor!* You want to know everything. You pressure me with so many demands. If you could, and we let you, you'd overwhelm me, to make me say certain things that I consider it an obligation, out of loyalty, to keep in the utmost secrecy. Poor Sacha, this innocent little boy of mine, a child at the time, a little nincompoop who was still unaware of the wickedness of the world, suffered more than you could know. It was the first in a long chain of defeats he's known in life. I'm not going to snitch on someone just to satisfy the morbid curiosity of any random lout. Those armoires, mind you, are full of papers. It took Karapetiz years to interpret some phenomena, and you want to know everything at once. Why should I give you the pleasure? Because of your pretty face? So that a tremendous idler doesn't have to make the slightest effort! Do you want me to start looking for the paper you need right now? Translate the fundamental pages for you? From what language into what language?' I defended myself as best I could. I made it clear to her that I wasn't demanding anything, that I had no desire to see those papers. I only dared to ask how the feast had ended, and, you can believe me, I'd broached that topic with the utmost innocence. 'The feast?' she exclaimed in astonishment. 'Have you the nerve to consider that disgrace a feast? Feast? A feast, that heap of filth? I'm beginning to realize, my friend, that your morals are rather loosey-goosey! That performance, if you'd really like to know, ended when all the men present married all the women present, gave them many children, and on Sundays took them to sunbathe on the beach. You don't believe me? Well, I'll tell you the truth, it ended when the faithful said their last prayers, lit a candle in memory of their Holy Child, and went quietly off to take a nap. The learned Aram Karapetiz, your humble servant; her brother, the halfwit present here, a good-for-nothing, a nonentity—despite finding me full of benevolence!—and his so-called friend Tagalong, whom he picked up who knows where, tourist guide and professional adventurer, two-bit pimp, debaucher, swine, had to take I don't know how many naps to recover from that atrocious experience, in your home, located in the centrally located Calle de La Palma, number ninety-five, apartment seven, a humble but honorable home, where one could indeed sleep, and not in that shitty field where not even the pigs dared to wallow. But tell me! Why do you want to know these things, mere scientific interest? You're crazy if you think I'll buy that song and dance!' She looked at me with a baleful eye. A twitch in her right eyelid began to distort her toucan-like face. 'I've already told you what came next was frightening. Isn't my word enough for you? You ask me too much. Have you forgotten that you are dealing with a lady? A lady! Are you going to demand that I take a shit in front of you too?' The situation, as you may have noticed, had become untenable. Marietta Karapetiz lifted her black dress above her knees and proceeded to squat down, just as Ramona had done minutes before. Her face was distorted with anger, contempt, disgust. 'Forgive me!' I said with all the dignity I could muster. 'I haven't, nor have I ever had, the slightest interest in knowing that abominable story.' Omar and the fat servant helped her up from the floor and sat her in a chair. 'It was you who insisted on telling it.' And then, with the most casual expression it was possible for me to adopt, I looked at my watch and added: 'Look at that! Ladies and gentlemen, I've wasted so much of your precious time! I hadn't the slightest idea that it was so late! I must say goodnight.' I was determined, no matter what, even at the risk of Sacha breaking my ribs, that I had to escape."

The doorbell rang.

Amelia Millares got up and opened the door. A man in a uniform introduced himself as the Licenciado De la Estrella's chauffeur. He said that since that morning he'd been sure that things were going to end on a bad note. With a commanding tone, he told his employer that it was time to be on their way, to stop clowning around, that this was the last time, he swore, that he was going to drive him home in this state.

"Just a moment, Arnulfo, just a moment and I'll be at your disposal! I've arrived almost at the end. I swear it won't happen to me this time, Arnulfo, I swear, it won't be necessary to clean me up. Millares, tell him to let me stay a few minutes! Tell him how well I've behaved. I can't get up now." And without any transition, he continued: "That group, surprised by my assertiveness, failed to react for a moment. They watched me move toward the door in silence. Steel Grip didn't even attempt to stop me. When I'd already opened the door, and had one foot outside, I turned to the group and asked provocatively, 'So how did that filthy coven end? I can well imagine, but I'd rather hear it from your own lips!' The sister and brother were bewildered, all confidence lost. Marietta Karapetiz began to mumble in a submissive voice: 'Look, a frail, little old women showed me her offering on a beautiful white porcelain plate. I was frightened at the sight of how much that tiny body was able to hold. She approached the Holy Child ... They made us kneel ... Please, señor, I beg you, don't force me to go on! I'm a very old woman. I've suffered much. I lost my parents as a mere infant. My poor heart is no longer what it was. I regret having known you.' She took a deep breath. At that instant, as if by a miracle, she seemed to regain all her lost strength. With a booming voice that a sergeant would envy, she shouted, 'Get out of here! Get out of here, right now! Sacha, for God's sake, do something, get him out of here, as only you can!' I didn't wait any longer. I closed the door and ran down the stairs. I didn't want to take the elevator for fear of an unwelcome surprise. As I stepped out onto the street, I heard my name being called and raised my head. The old bawd and the whole unsavory lot of miscreants had come out onto the balcony. Their shouts turned into squawks. Sacha was showing me my raincoat and hat and motioning with one hand for me to come up and get them. Come up? No way in hell! I shouted for them to throw down my clothes. I searched for a word, the one that would wound them the most, to hurl at them as soon as I had my things in my hand. I thought I saw something metallic shining on the balcony. Something brushed my temples, something hit me on a shoulder. I looked up and saw Marietta Karapetiz and Sacha emptying chamber pots on top of me. Just then the worst possible thing happened. Zuleima, Omar, and the adipose youth emptied a large basin full of waste on me. I tried to run away and couldn't. I slipped; most of the contents fell on me. I heard a roar of laughter, indecent screams, hooting and hollering. I'd been left on all fours like a pig, wallowing in slippery, disgusting matter. I'd lost my glasses. I struggled as best I could, fell down another couple of times, and hit myself badly. I don't know where I wandered or for how long. I looked for the sea but didn't find it. Several hours went by about which I know nothing. I arrived at the hotel that night in a police car. An employee identified me as a guest and threw a blanket over me, because I was wearing nothing but underwear. Surely they'd taken off my dirty clothes and put me in a shower at the police station. They made me enter through a service entrance. The policeman who accompanied me returned my passport. I went up to my room. Someone informed me that two hours earlier Rodrigo Vives had been admitted to a clinic. I packed my bags, but the reception desk informed me that I would only be allowed to take it with me if I paid the bill. Fortunately, in the room, I'd retrieved a few dollars, not many, I'd hidden in the lining of my suitcase. I explained that I was a guest of the Viveses; were it up to me, I would never in my goddamn life have set foot, not only in their hotel, but in their entire country. My wallet had disappeared along with my dirty suit. They called the police station, which explained that I'd been picked up in the street wearing only my underwear. It couldn't be true. Where had my passport come from then? Anyway, I left my suitcase, sold my watch and fountain pen for a starvation price to a clerk, walked to the station, and didn't move from there until my train left. I traveled in a state of semiconsciousness; the only thing I was able to register was the stench, perhaps imaginary, that my body gave off. Rodrigo Vives never sent me the suitcase. I thought of filing a lawsuit. Not only had I been robbed of my belongings, but I'd suffered severe emotional harm. But to go to court in a foreign country is to fight a losing battle. I had to wait until I got to Mexico before I saw a cent. Oh, but before that I'd already met the famous María Inmaculada de la Concepción; I tried my luck and came out on bottom there too."

The storyteller lost his breath again. He was gasping like a fish about to drown. He arched his body and became frozen in a state of unnatural rigor. He began to give off a repellent stench. The Millares walked silently away from the putrid object. The chauffeur took charge of transporting him to the car. Don Antonio Millares went out into the garden with his grandchildren.

"Did you notice . . . ?" he asked Juan Ramón, without knowing how to end the question.

"Yes," was the grandson's laconic reply. After walking for another while, Juan Ramón asked in turn: "What should a man do when that happens to him?"

"When what happens to him?"

At that moment a flash of lightning lit up the mountain. A clap of thunder was heard in the distance. Grandfather didn't hear his grandson's answer. They walked on in silence.

Funchal, April 1987
Prague, March 1988

Sergio Pitol (1933–2018) was one of Mexico's most influential and respected literary figures. A native of Veracruz, he studied law and philosophy in Mexico City and enjoyed a long and distinguished diplomatic career, first as a cultural attaché in Mexican embassies and consulates across the globe, including Poland, Hungary, Italy, and China, and ultimately as ambassador to the former Czechoslovakia. The author of numerous novels, short stories, and volumes of criticism, he was also a renowned translator of some of the nineteenth and twentieth century's most celebrated works of literature, by authors as diverse as James, Conrad, Gombrowicz, Chekov, Austen, and Pilnyak. Having begun publishing in the 1960s, he was an influential contemporary of the foundational authors of the Latin American "Boom." In recognition of the significance and scope of his entire canon of work, Pitol was awarded the two most important prizes in the Spanish-speaking world: the Juan Rulfo Prize in 1999 (now known as the FIL Literary Award in Romance Languages) and in 2005 the Cervantes Prize, commonly referred to as the "Spanish-language Nobel."

George Henson is the author of ten book-length translations, including works by Cervantes laureates Sergio Pitol (published by Deep Vellum) and Elena Poniatowska. His translations have appeared variously in *Words Without Borders*, *Asymptote*, *Latin American Literature Today*, *World Literature Today*, *Granta*, *Two Lines*, and the *New England Review*. He holds a PhD from the University of Texas at Dallas and is an adjunct professor of Spanish translation at the Middlebury Institute of International Studies in Monterey and of creative writing at the University of Tulsa. George is a 2021–2023 Tulsa Artist Fellow in literary translation.